A collection of tales of tomorrow

CW00841007

Also in Scholastic Press:

Out of the Mouths of Babes
Dennis Hamley

Criss Cross
Susan Gates

Unquiet Spirits
K. M. Peyton

TECHNOFEAR

A collection of tales of tomorrow

Laurence Staig

SCHOLASTIC
PRESS

For Clare Conville
(Agent provocateur?)

Scholastic Children's Books,
Commonwealth House, 1-19 New Oxford Street,
London WC1A 1NU, UK
a division of Scholastic Ltd
London ~ New York ~ Toronto ~ Sydney ~ Auckland

First published in the UK by Scholastic Ltd, 1997

Copyright © Laurence Staig, 1997

ISBN 0 590 54230 3

Typeset by DP Photosetting, Aylesbury, Bucks.
Printed by Cox and Wyman Ltd, Reading, Berks.

10 9 8 7 6 5 4 3 2 1

All rights reserved

The right of Laurence Staig to be identified as the author of this work has
been asserted by him in accordance with the Copyright, Designs and
Patents Act, 1988.

This book is sold subject to the condition that it shall not, by way of trade or
otherwise, be lent, resold, hired out, or otherwise circulated without the
publisher's prior consent in any form of binding or cover other than that
in which it is published and without a similar condition, including this
condition, being imposed upon the subsequent purchaser.

Contents

"Never let the future disturb you."
Marcus Aurelius

Lottery

"You're so damn suave!" exclaimed Jenny. Her tongue licked the top of her lip as though removing a smidgeon of cream.

Barry leaned forward across the table, straining to look at the numbers for himself. Above them the sounds of the *Weekly Fortune* TV show continued its drone of never-ending word-fodder. On the screen a glitter-suited presenter was calling out numbers, written on cards which were handed to him by a tame chimpanzee. Occasionally, the numbers would flash along the bottom of the screen. It was Lottery night.

"Ah-ha," said Jess, as he pulled the slip of paper closer to his chest, protectively ensuring that none of the others could see what was printed there. He flicked his orange fringe back and looked at the others down his long nose. He peeked at his slip of paper once more and grinned.

"That's four times in . . . in. . ." began Barry.

"In two months, isn't it, Jess?" Jenny butted in with a smile. She pushed her face towards Jess and switched on her *do-you-like-me?* eyes.

"That's right," he said, with more than a touch of

smugness. "It's simply that some us have got it, and some, well, some of us ain't."

He directed this last remark at Barry, who skulked back into his seat. His hang-dog, basset-hound face fell into place, but just like an excited puppy, he would bound back again.

From the rear of the café came the clatter of hurriedly collected cups and saucers. Nearby, three elderly dossers were gathered in the corner by the counter. That was one disadvantage of this place: they seemed to have some kind of social conscience and let *anyone* in. But it was also the only place that would put up with Jess and his entourage – with their reputation they couldn't be fussy. One dosser in particular appeared to ignore the excitement of Jess and his friends, choosing instead to slowly sip luke-warm coffee. He gazed myopically at a copy of yesterday's newspaper, which somebody had left stuffed behind the seat. Occasionally, his brow would furrow and he would glance at them over the top of the paper, just like some kind of businessman. The second dosser looked half-asleep, his eyelids near to closing. The third simply sat silently and watched the kids' antics. He had seen one of them before: a nasty piece of work who had viciously kicked his friend George, when his only crime had been to shelter in the doorway of some posh restaurant when it was raining.

The young blonde waitress, with the close-cropped hair, stopped chewing on the stale gum she had popped into her mouth hours earlier. Curiosity was getting the better of her. She decided to take an interest in the cause of the earlier cheering and exchanges of congratulations. Then she noticed that "he" was still there, the boy with the orange-tinted hair who every one of the staff disliked. She sniffed for a moment, wondering whether to try and ignore them; he had made a pass at her more than once. But there was no getting away from it, he seemed to have the devil's own luck and the occasional Saturday night visits to the café to check his Lottery tickets confirmed it.

Jess looked up suddenly. He noticed that she had stopped collecting the cups and was looking directly at him.

"Hey – waitress, you! Come here!"

She froze for a second, unsure whether to respond with some put-down to his command, or whether to go with the moment and see what would happen. She put her saucers down on the table and licked a new sheet into place on her order pad. Returning his glance, she crossed the floor to their table.

"We're celebrating, fresh coffees all round! Make them cappuccinos with lots of chocolate on the top, we only had a dash of the stuff last time."

"My," she smirked as she took her pencil out of her apron pocket. "More coffee? You certainly know how to live, bet you've seen it all, eh?"

The corner of her mouth curled as she scribbled the order on to her pad.

"Jess has won some more dosh on the Lottery!" beamed Barry. "We're celebrating, ain't we, Jess?"

"How much?" asked the waitress.

"Sorry?" Jess pulled a face in disbelief at her nerve.

"How much?" repeated the waitress. "Are we talking two or three million, or what?"

"That's none of your business!" said Jess.

"Couple of hundred, ain't it, Jess?"

Jenny rolled her eyes upwards. Her brother was such a motor-mouth, she'd never get anywhere with Jess as long as he insisted on tagging along. But she had promised to keep an eye on him.

Jess snorted and brushed the sleeves of his jacket, as though he were about to leave the foyer of some exclusive London club.

The waitress resumed chewing her gum and raised an eyebrow.

"Going to buy yourself a couple of yachts, then?"

Jess seethed. Jenny glanced at him anxiously.

"Take no notice of her, Jess," she said. "Probably just jealous."

Behind them came the tinkle of a cup being replaced in its saucer. A gruff-sounding voice cleared its throat.

"Aren't you too young to do that?"

The waitress turned on her heels to face the old dosser who had been reading. He had lowered his paper and was staring at them.

"I said, aren't you too young to do that Lottery thing, to gamble."

"Ignore him," said Jess. "They shouldn't allow people like him in here."

4

"Oh, yeah," whined Barry. "*Too young* – so what! Maybe he is, but Jess looks older and he gets his Lottery tickets out of those dispensers at the supermarkets! His dad don't mind – gives him loads of dosh to play with. He always wins on things, fruit machines, you name it – just about anything!"

Jenny kicked Barry beneath the table. Jess shot a look of thunder at the dosser, who remained calm and unperturbed. His eyes were hard as steel, but they masked a touch of humour that was betrayed by laughter lines gathered in other places on his face. He had a generous, pure white beard, but his hair was still dark. The half-asleep dosser who sat beside him nudged him with his elbow.

"Just mind your own business, Santa Claus," said Jess, trying to return and better the edge of his gaze.

The dosser laughed, long and low; he exchanged a smile with his companions.

"Santa Claus, indeed! Now then, aren't you the one who's in the privileged position of Santa Claus? I mean, a young man of wealth, winning all that money and all?"

Jenny sat closer to Jess and whispered in his ear. "Wait for it – he'll ask for a hand-out, I betcha, his type always do."

Jess's stare remained.

True to Jenny's warning, the old dosser opened his palm and spat in it. He laughed and rubbed both of his hands together, and then extended a greeting. Jess wrinkled his nose and made a noise of obvious disgust.

5

"It's for luck, lad. This has been the first cup of hot stuff me and the boys have had for days. All due to the kindness of this lass here. Can you spare us a meal? Come and shake me hand, I promise you that you'll be luckier still."

"Shake hands with yourself, then," snapped Jess.

With that he turned to the waitress.

"Like I said, bring us some coffee and step on it. I suppose a dump like this hasn't got anything decent for us to eat."

The waitress sighed and was about to reel off the usual fare when the dosser rose to his feet. Jess shuffled awkwardly, fearing he might be starting something.

"Whatever they have we don't mind, perhaps you could give us the price of a meal or something? Or maybe just a small round of sandwiches?" He reached out his hand again. "If the food here's not to your taste, then think of us. We're travellers, we're men of the road, and we haven't eaten for some while."

"We can do a sausage sandwich," said the waitress helpfully, preparing to add the order to her pad.

Barry ran his fingers through what little remained of his disastrous semi-shaven haircut, and jumped up and down in his seat.

"Sausage sandwich! Ha ha ha! You're talking to Jess Mannering here – Jess is *the* man. He's your top dude, man of style, of class. Jess only eats the best at the best."

Jenny thumped her brother in the ribs.

"Jess is a bit of a gourmet," she said, snootily.

"Then, lad," the dosser continued, "if that's the case, and this place isn't the grand gaff you're used to..." He paused and allowed a huge smile to crack across his face. He gave the waitress a wink. "Then, why are you here?"

Jess looked uncomfortable. How could he explain that there were not too many cafés around here that would admit him and his friends. Especially him. His reputation as the ultimate pain in the ass, the most self-opinionated and privileged brat in the town had long gone before him. Restaurant and café managers for miles around declared they were full when they saw him approach. His stockbroker father had the same reputation, and "like father like son", as the manager of the Golden Kitchen had once remarked.

Jess swallowed and cast his eyes down to the table, hoping a suitable excuse or explanation would spring to mind.

"I mean, I can see you have class," the dosser continued, clearly getting into his stride now. "I bet you come from a family used to fine things?"

Barry nodded furiously; his sister gritted her teeth. Jess felt anger welling up inside. Finally he looked up – but this time he ignored the man and smiled over-pleasantly at the waitress.

"Coffees – cappuccinos – as I asked."

She nodded and turned.

"Oh, and waitress." He clicked his fingers. "Bring me three plates and a packet of peanuts."

The girl frowned. Jess remained stone-faced. Barry looked up at him, his eyes wide in admiration and wonder, and began to giggle.

After a moment, she returned with the plates and a small silver-foiled packet. Jess tore open the corner and counted three peanuts into his hand. Carefully, and with a flourish, he placed a single nut on each of the three plates, then threw back his head and swallowed the rest in a single gulp. Barry slapped the surface of the table with his hand. This was a huge joke! Jess was so bloody damn suave.

The dosser watched him, his amiable smile dissolving, but he remained calm. Jess pushed the plates towards him and made a huge mocking gesture with a wave of his hand.

"Please, be my guest. Although they might be nicer barbecued."

The café fell silent. Through the serving hatch behind the counter, even the kitchen staff were watching, their mouths partially open in wonder. Barry gulped, fearing that Jess might have gone too far.

Instead of any cacophony of protest breaking out, the third dosser, who had been sitting silently in the background, observing all, stood up. He was a tall man; normally he would shave as he wore only a few days' stubble on his chin. He had deep brown eyes, dark slots in his face which made it difficult to exchange his gaze. Silently, he crossed to their table where the plates lay, and picked up two and offered them to his companions. Then took the third himself.

"I'd like to thank you, young sir, on behalf of my colleagues here. We seldom know such kindness."

With that he bowed and returned to his seat. Barry and Jenny allowed an audible sigh of relief to escape.

The tall man picked up his peanut and nibbled at it as if it were some kind of delicacy. Afterwards, he flicked a crumb from his mouth and turned to the dosser with the white beard.

"You know, O'Hara, I was wondering whether our young host here, with his interest in gaming machines, the high life and good food and the like, I was wondering whether he'd be interested in that place we happened upon a while back."

Jess cocked his head to one side.

The bearded dosser's eyes flicked wider.

"Where would that be?"

"Oh," continued the tall man, "you must remember. Less than a hundred miles from here – over in the east, that town in the marshlands."

"Oh! Yes, of course – you mean *that* place."

The three of them grinned like monkeys, the dosser with the beard beginning to smile with more enthusiasm.

"I mean, a young man interested in the fineries of life would hardly believe his luck, walking into Arkham. And their barbecue is legendary."

"Ah yes," said the third dosser, speaking at last.

"Arkham – we certainly had the best meal I have ever tasted in my life there. Few people know about the place, do they? A shame that, a real shame."

"And," butted in the bearded dosser, "there was all the fun of getting it!"

"Yes," said his friend. "All the fun of getting it. Their Lottery machines – in every café and restaurant, newsagent – everywhere. Beautiful pieces of machinery, sparkling steel and chrome. Little works of art on every street corner!"

"What do you mean, 'fun of getting it'?" Jenny had been listening.

"Oh yes," he said, coldly. "There was all the fun of getting the best meal you'll *ever taste in your life.*"

The last part of his sentence had been spoken with emphasis. Jess's ears pricked up. He turned slowly towards the three dossers. The waitress appeared with their coffees, but with a wave of his hand he directed that they should now be placed on the dossers' table. The tall man bowed. Jess still wasn't sure whether he was being mocked.

"Arkham really enjoys their Lottery. It's their own, you see, but the prize is beyond your wildest imagination, beyond your wildest dreams."

"It surely is that, lad." The dosser with the beard raised his coffee in salutation.

Once again a strange silence fell over the café. The three old men sat on their bench as though they were ancient wraiths, waiting and watching with a wisdom known only to themselves. Jess felt distinctly uncomfortable, and Barry – who usually had to be restrained – had become calm and quiet.

Jess rose to his feet and gestured to the waitress to follow him across to the other side of the café. She hesitated at first, but there was an insistent look about him. He really wanted to speak to her, and in private.

He reached into his wallet and pulled out a note, which he pushed into her hand. Then he leaned towards her ear.

"Those three scumbags, do they come here a lot?"

She frowned. "Sometimes, not often; they travel about a bit, I think."

"Do you know of this place, this Arkham?"

She looked past him. Jess's friends were watching them, but the three dossers seemed unperturbed, choosing instead to drink their benefactor's offering.

"Yeah. I've heard them speak of the town once or twice, not that often. It's a remote place out in the Fens somewhere; you know, the marshlands out in the east."

"What are they on about with this thing about the food?"

"Nothing great, no big deal, just that it's got a reputation for good restaurants. And..." She paused.

"Yes, yes what else?"

The waitress smiled and then sighed.

"Like I said, no big deal – just something about a Lottery, they run their own Lottery – mad about it, but that's all I know."

Jess looked thoughtful, then nodded.

A town with its own Lottery and good food? Perhaps he'd treat himself – a day or two away. Why not?

When he returned to his seat he found it difficult to remain. The tall dosser was sat with an almost permanent grin on his face, and somehow his dark eyes seemed to have receded into the skull-like topography of his face.

The train journey there had been pleasant enough, although Jess's steak had not been cooked properly, and of course he had complained. This had resulted in a terrible rumpus in the dining-car.

For a while the scenery had been varied and interesting, then after about forty minutes the variety began to fade. Familiar streets and buildings became displaced by a seemingly endless vista of flat grey wilderness. The line at which the sky met the earth was straighter than a ruler's edge. Black tarn patches pitted the seamless blanket of mottled moonscape. An occasional figure broke the monotony; Jess thought they might be scarecrows as they stood in fields – but why should scarecrows wave? Although the train had sped past what seemed to be farmland, it occured to Jess that he had seen very few animals – if any at all.

When the train stopped at Marshfen station, Jess wondered where on earth he had arrived. He was the only passenger to step on to the platform, and at first he wondered whether his intended adventure was a mistake. The station looked abandoned, the few buildings that were not vandalized seemed as though they had been captured in time.

He shivered, a cold wind blew his fringe, and the other-worldly moan of it caused him to glance over his shoulder. This was not like him, and part of him felt angry for his inexplicable nervousness.

The station office was deserted, but through the dirt-smeared windows of the station doors he saw a solitary car, with a lop-sided cracked sign on its roof: TAXI.

In the driver's seat sat a figure, stuffed large by several woolly jumpers and a red scarf which he had tucked down his front. Wire-framed spectacles, one arm twisted, were perched on the tip of his nose. He was reading a paper, and the sound of Jess's foot-steps made him grudgingly look up and peer out of his window. He seemed suprised that anyone had aligh-ted.

"Cab, sir?" he said, quietly.

Jess looked about him. In the distance he saw a spire, and the red and brown rooftops of assorted buildings. They looked a compact collection, as though they were toys in a model village. To the right, some way further apart, there seemed to be a cluster of strange shapes: a mixture of ovals and triangles which sagged, proving difficult to make out what they were exactly. He imagined from what appeared to be a perimeter fence that it might be some military installation. On either side of these structures was nothing except for an occasional figure he assumed to be a scarecrow. Above this was space and bleak, huddled clouds.

"Cab, sir?" said the driver, again.

Jess was pulled back to earth. The landscape had seemed hypnotic. The town looked out of place. It reminded him of a growth on the earth.

"Is that Arkham?" he asked, pointing towards the spire.

"It is, sir."

"Then that's where I want to go."

The driver folded his paper and looked him up and down. Jess might have been mistaken, but just for a moment he thought that he detected a rising sense of uncertainty, almost protestation, about his request.

"Is . . . is there an address, sir?"

"No, I just want to see the place."

The driver glanced downwards and cleared his throat.

"To *see* the place!" The driver laughed.

"I'm just a visitor – for the day, perhaps two. I gather they have good restaurants."

He shot Jess a look which alarmed him, and for a moment, the driver said nothing.

"I can take you to the edge of town, sir, no further."

Jess was about to protest, then thought better of it. This man clearly had some problem, and it wasn't worth pursuing. After all, he was a tourist today, a gourmet in search of excellence. He opened the rear door, and climbed in.

The taxi driver dropped him at the corner of a high wall

which led to a row of terraced cottages. These, he had said, formed a corridor into the centre of the place. From a distance Jess had thought that Arkham looked sombre. As they neared the edge of town he was able to see the nature of the buildings better. The even strata of brown rooftops, with their moss patchwork of intermingled green hues, had appeared strangely depressing. He imagined that this was going to be an old town, an ancient town full of gumbo-faced natives with wide, vacant expressions.

The reality was quite different.

His driver had been silent throughout the journey. Ordinarily Jess would have been glad about this, not having to listen to the usual mindless drivel about the weather or the state of the nation. But on this occasion the silence had served to reinforce his sense of uncertainty about his quest. Was it a quest after all? He paused and took a deep breath before he made his way around the corner and into Arkham.

A wonderland of serenity unfolded before him, and being unprepared for what he saw, he lurched backwards and almost swallowed a laugh.

It was as if he had been dropped into a scene from a Disney movie. There were no cartoon characters, but instead there was the kind of street scene where all is clearly sugar and spice, Mary Poppins land, a sickeningly goody-goody world. Trees lined the street, bearing copious clusters of lily-white blossom. There were neat front gardens, and their owners were busy watering and tending to the islands of different flower beds which were a feature of every house. These gardens either led down to the pavements in an open border, or there was the occasional white picket fence, obviously newly painted. To his right a young man with a paintbrush was applying a new coat of gloss to his fence. He nodded at Jess and declared, "What a nice day!"

And the birdsong!

It seemed to be everywhere; swallows swooped and dived, as though they were dancing their way along the main street. The road was cobbled, and there wasn't a car in sight. To his left a cyclist was carefully and slowly weaving her way amongst the pedestrians, some of whom bore open parasols, all similarly patterned in a rainbow mixture of colours. The message *A Lottery ticket eases our burden* had been emblazoned around the border.

Jess stepped forward. He passed a too-brightly painted postbox, and a small group of children who appeared to be happily playing a game against a fence; it was either marbles or jacks, something he hadn't seen for years.

Nearby, an elderly lady appeared at her front door and waved at him.

"Good morning, beautiful day!"

Jess nodded and waved back – he couldn't help himself. He stopped for a second to take it all in. The streets gleamed like polished furnishings. Everything sparkled, the doorknobs, the letterboxes and even the streetlamps. A pure-white Persian cat sat smugly on a street bench, purring and allowing the emerging warmth of an unexpected sun to soothe and pacify.

A voice called out from behind him. Jess thought at first someone was speaking to him, but he was mistaken. Instead a passer-by had been addressed by an elderly man uncoiling a garden hose.

"Hi, Jack! Got yours yet?" he called.

The pedestrian waved a newspaper in acknowledgement. "Still got two scratchcards left!"

"Well done!" came the reply.

Jess suddenly felt warm and assured deep down inside. With a reborn inner confidence, he walked on.

At the end of the street was a junction. A glance to his right revealed a town square in which a magnificent fountain spouted an ever-changing gush of crystal-clear, blue-tinged frothy water. A small queue had formed nearby. Jess wondered whether they were queueing to post letters, or perhaps they were standing in front of an especially popular vending machine of some kind, but after just a few moments the line shrank and he was able to see more clearly.

A young woman placed a coin into a slot just above the thin black slit in the upper trunk of the contraption. Jess remembered the dosser's words at the café: *"Beautiful pieces of machinery, sparkling steel and chrome. Little works of art on every street corner!"* The line had been for Lottery tickets.

He noticed a poster on a nearby lamp-post. It had been pasted on to the front of a sheet of hardboard. *The Arkham Lottery: promoted by your town council.*

Help keep our streets clean and clear. Preserve the Arkham heritage.

Jess nodded in approval. Now he understood. This was the reason why everywhere was so clean and fresh and wholesome. He scanned the pavements around him; there was not a sweet wrapper or a cigarette butt in sight. The paving stones were as smooth and unblemished as silver dinner platters. He smelt the air: it was honey and wild grass, with just a hint of something wonderful cooking somewhere.

"This is what it should be like," he said, under his breath. "A place with standards, a town that takes pride in its streets and thoroughfares."

A number of other passers-by smiled and acknowledged him. One even called him "Friend". Jess continued across the square. Groups of people were chattering, dogs wagged their tails and the birdsong continued as if it would explode into the very air around him. He was guided by his nose; he sniffed the air again, this time almost reaching up on tiptoe to solve the mystery of what it could be.

"Ahh! Lovely, isn't it?"

He turned on his heels and saw a young girl beside him. Without a further word she reached into her basket and pulled out a white rose. Cocking her head to one side she broke the stem and inserted the rose into his lapel.

"Be sure to get your ticket now!" she said, and moved into the crowd.

Jess's jaw dropped. For a moment he wondered

whether he might be dreaming; she was a pure vision, but within minutes she had disappeared.

"This is heaven," he said.

In the centre of the square a group of trestle-tables and benches had been arranged beside a platform. He thought that the smell might be coming from this direction and went to investigate. A group of men in white overalls and hats were busy clearing a brick bed of ashes, above which was a long iron rod on a mechanical winch. One of the men was cleaning the rod, shaving the remains of what Jess presumed to be meat from a spit. This was collected into a bucket. One of the men noticed that he was watching them.

"Morning," said the man.

"Morning to you," said Jess. "Is that the delicious smell I can detect? Is it a barbecue?"

"Indeed, as you must know, it's barbecue this month. It were pies last month, it'll be stew next month!"

He glanced up at his companions and they all broke out into a laugh. Jess joined them.

"I'm visiting," Jess continued. "I'd heard about the cuisine here."

"The cuisine? Oh yes, it's excellent, we have that reputation."

"So – when are you having the barbecue, then?"

The man sniffed and wiped his brow.

"Tonight. Result of the draw. Got yourself a ticket?"

"No, no, not yet." Jess felt suddenly excited at the prospect.

"Oh, you must get one. Come to the square tonight and see if your number comes up. It's announced, there's a bit of a do. Then we have the barbecue, cooked by the town's chef – the great Monsieur Grillet, from France. It's a delight to see. The food is out-standing."

One of the other men, who had begun to arrange bricks of charcoal beneath a metal grid, joined them.

"Morning – tourist, eh?"

Jess nodded. The men smiled.

"Have you heard of our Monsieur Grillet?"

"No – but I'd love to taste one of his dishes!"

The men nodded. The man who had been cleaning the spit threw his knife into a nearby tray.

"See across there? Behind the fountain?"

Jess peered across the square. There were a small line of shops, but in the centre was a canopy above a small cluster of circular tables.

"That's his restaurant. Magnificent! If you've any doubts about his ability to prepare a barbecue fit for the angels, go and have a bite there – just something light."

Jess needed little persuading.

"Why yes, yes, why not? Thank you!"

"Hurry now, he'll only be open for another hour; they will be preparing for the special tonight."

Jess thanked them and turned towards the canopy.

"Don't forget your ticket!" someone called after him, and as he made his way between the gathering crowd he could hear the music of their cheery laughter in the distance.

The meal had been pure nectar. Jess had chosen pancakes with a filling that had dissolved in his mouth, leaving an aftertaste of bliss. He now decided just to shoot the breeze, and had ordered his favourite after-lunch coffee whilst he watched the passing of time in the square. This certainly was the place to be. The Lottery machine remained busy, with eager Arkham residents plying its greedy mouth with coins.

Jess moved a chair across from a nearby table, put his feet up and settled more comfortably into his seat. A very polite waitress brought him his bill. This was so different to the miserable cafés and restaurants he frequented back home. For a moment he closed his eyes and breathed the scented air.

All of a sudden, his descent into ultimate relaxation was rudely interrupted. From somewhere to his left he heard the sound of a woman's voice, shrieking, "He went that way!" Jess opened one eye and shifted in his seat. A small crowd tumbled into his view. A blend of angry voices filled the air, and somebody cried out, "Over there, officer!"

The angry squawl of a siren cut through the air like a knife. Jess lowered his feet to the floor and leant forward. The crowd had gathered around a young man, dressed raggedly in a stained beige raincoat tied with string. A woollen bobble cap was perched far back on his head, and he held what seemed to be a strap, or maybe a dog's lead, in one of his hands. His eyes were wide and terrified.

"Ma dog, I los' ma dog. Thought he may have come ta' town! Didn't mean to come here!"

A large man, dressed in blue with a peaked cap, appeared on the scene and cut his way through the crowd.

"Now, my lad, you've got your place, you know full well what your place is! You know the rules!"

"Ma dog, mister, he ran away. I'm sorry, won't come again!"

Another uniformed figure appeared, a woman with two stripes on her arm with the word "Security" in golden threaded letters just below.

"It's all right, folks, no need for alarm, no harm done. He was only looking for his dog, we'll see he gets back to the compound, don't want to spoil your day."

Within minutes the crowd dispersed. Jess could hear their comments, which ranged from "Shocking," to "How disgraceful – they have their place. It's not as if we don't look after them."

Jess was fascinated.

"You must be a tourist?" said a voice.

Jess looked up. His waitress had returned and was watching the commotion with him.

"Yes, yes I am," he said.

Suddenly it occurred to him. He hadn't seen a single dosser, homeless person or street peddler since his arrival. For a brief moment he puzzled over this, since it had been a group of dossers who had told him about the town in the first place.

"They said something about a compound?"

"Yes," said the girl. "Of course. We are very street-proud, we have a strong sense of civic pride here; we are known for it!"

"Yes, of course." Jess was impressed. They had managed to rid their streets of scum. No wonder everything was so neat and tidy, so pleasant.

"You have a place for street people?" he asked.

"The raggedy people? Certainly. They have their own camp on the edge of town."

Jess remembered the place with the wire fencing he had seen on his way in. He had mistaken some kind of dossers refuge for a military set-up. Jess was becoming more impressed as each moment passed. This town had clearly got itself sorted out.

"Did you enjoy your meal?" the waitress asked.

Jess smiled. "It was wonderful, simply amazing. I'm something of a gourmet, you know. Very particular about what I eat. And, er, where. My compliments on your town."

"Why, thank you. Are you coming into the square tonight?"

"The, the..."

"The Lottery!" she laughed. "Oh, you must come! It's a wonderful night, we have fireworks, too. Be sure to get your ticket, there's a machine on every corner!"

"Yes, yes. Why not?"

Jess spent the rest of his day wandering the streets of

paradise. Everything was so proper, and true to the dosser's words, it was entirely a town of fine restaurants and good living; they were to be found down every street. He easily passed the time by reading the menus which were displayed in restaurant windows. An old news-stand sheet announced last week's Lottery winner: *Grand Barbecue Night a Success!* Arkham seemed to have cracked its social problems, with the simple expediency of shuffling them off elsewhere.

There was indeed a Lottery machine on every street corner; they were fine-looking reminders to the people of Arkham of their social responsibility. And now he began to notice the large number of civic posters, too, which reminded townsfolk that their Lottery ticket bought them peace of mind. He noticed the regularity of their recurring motto: "A Lottery ticket eases our burden".

He had bought five tickets for himself. Now he was almost salivating at the prospect of possibly winning, and the prize, what a prize! A fantastic barbecue prepared by Monsieur Grillet himself! He had already decided to stay for a couple of days longer, and he thought he might stay at the hotel which overlooked the square near the fountain.

The excitement of the approach of the evening was unmistakable. There was an electricity in the air which crackled and fizzed, as the townsfolk of Arkham hurried about like drones. Jess could not resist allowing himself to be caught up in the atmosphere. By seven o'clock the square was filling with people, more benches had been put out and some early arrivals had even brought picnic baskets and rugs.

Jess ordered himself a large milkshake and ice-cream from a street parlour which had been recommended, and sat at a little table and watched the preparations.

The stage was now dressed with generously filled baskets of flowers. The barbecue was already underway, and as the purple sheen of the evening sky crept over the square, the warm, comforting glow of the coals and charcoal marked it as the centre of attention. Balloons of different colours – silver and gold, blues and oranges – were all around him. Some of the audience had paper hats with the words *Arkham Lottery* across the band. To the right, a small ensemble of brass players added to the thrill of the occasion.

Jess was enjoying himself. He searched for his tickets, which he removed from his wallet to a more convenient place in his shirt pocket.

Behind him, the throaty roar and rumble of arriving vehicles rose above the excited cries of the townspeople. Their rattle and thrum suggested that they might be coaches. This was so much better than the Lottery on TV.

By eight o'clock the square was packed and the decline in the general murmur and conversation told him that they were about to begin. He swallowed hard in anticipation of a great evening.

The brass played a fanfare, the crowd rose to the occasion with whistles and cries. A spotlight picked out a fat man with slicked back hair and a gold lamé jacket.

"Ladies and gentleman, boys and girls, it's time. . . A Lottery ticket eases our burden! What does a Lottery ticket do?"

The crowd responded, bang on the mark.

"Eases our burden!" they sang.

A drum roll followed and then a smaller spotlight burst open, like a suddenly blossoming flower. Monsieur Grillet himself, his chef's hat cocked to one side, bounced on to the stage.

Immediately, a trolley was wheeled in front of him. On the top was a large plastic bubble, shaped like a goldfish bowl, and inside hundreds of small balls were furiously crashing around against the sides.

The fat man with the gold jacket lifted a microphone to his lips.

"OK, folks – as you know, we celebrate after the draw, so without any more ado, let's get this show on the road. One winner only, of course!"

The crowd laughed.

Monsieur Grillet placed his hand inside the bubble and withdrew a ball.

"Five!" said the fat man.

He removed another.

"Eight!" said the fat man again.

Another.

"Nine!"

The crowd roared, they were in an ecstasy of anticipation.

"Three!"

And then, one more.

"Seven! The winner, ladies and gentleman, boys and girls, is 58937! Who has that ticket?"

Jess's mouth dried. His hand shook as he removed his Lottery tickets from his pocket. He checked the first. That was no good. He checked the second – that was no good, either.

The crowd broke into a hum of conversation. Each person asking his or her neighbour if they had had any luck.

Jess checked his third ticket: 58937.

He felt dizzy, he reached out to steady himself as he rose from his table.

"Here! I've won!"

The fat man lifted the microphone to his mouth again. Lights flashed about him and somewhere a rocket shot into the cobalt sky, crackling open into a hundred silver showers of rain.

Suddenly, he felt someone grab his left arm, and immediately afterwards somebody else held his right. Before he could say anything further, two burly male members of the crowd were hurrying him towards the stage, and pushing him up the steps.

"Hey, hey, you guys!" Jess laughed. "Not so much enthusiasm!"

As he stood centre stage in the spotlight, wild applause and hoots broke out below. The fat man grabbed Jess's ticket and read out the number.

"I confirm. We have a winner! 58937 – this young man has won!"

Monsieur Grillet leaned forward and shook his hand. The fat man pushed his microphone into Jess's face.

"And you are?"

"My name is Jess Mannering!"

The crowd hooted and this time there were louder whistles and cries than before.

"And are you from Arkham?"

"No, no I'm a visitor, a tourist!"

The crowd went wild.

"Do you hear that, folks – we've got us a tourist! Thank God for that! My heartiest congratulations, young man. What an honour!"

Suddenly, Jess felt the grip on his arms again. But this time there was something else too. A rope was being threaded around him, and quickly pulled tight.

The fat man signalled to somebody at the back.

"OK – let them in!"

Jess was confused. His arms were bound tightly now, they hurt, and his two escorts held him fast. He peered through the gloom and watched in disbelief as another spotlight picked out a group of people who had gathered at the rear of the audience. A brown-coloured mass moved and sloped forward, as the crowd parted to allow it through. Another spotlight enabled him to see more clearly.

Dossers, dossers, and more dossers.

There were hundreds of them, ragged and dirty, unwashed and hungry. Their eyes were tiny eager specks, like anxious voles, and each and every one of them held a fork in their left hand.

Jess screamed.

He struggled to move his arms.

He felt sick, as a dark and awful realization struck him like a punch in the stomach.

The crowd heaved and whooped in support; they were going crazy.

Behind him a dozen rockets shot into the night. The band started up and Monsieur Grillet produced two fine carving knives, which he proceeded to sharpen on a stone before displaying the keeness of their edge to the audience.

As his two escorts raised him on to the barbecue, Jess noticed three particular faces amongst the dossers who were moving ever closer; they were at the front, eager and keen, and one had a pure-white beard. For seconds they were lit by the flares of the fireworks, their faces becoming ethereal, like angels. They had come for their feast.

He screamed again, failing to hear Monsieur Grillet's ever so polite enquiry to the bearded dosser as to how well cooked they would like their meat.

The Tingle

All of a sudden her leg jerked upwards again.

"Hey, that's really weird!" she squealed. "Come on now, stop it, I'm getting pins and needles in my knees!"

Margot LaStrange, the platinum-blonde reporter from the truly awful but wonderfully trendy *Yoof Edge* music magazine, twitched and twisted in her chair.

A tumble of bass notes rumbled around the sitting-room. The harmonic vibrated the empty glasses, which sat next to unwashed coffee mugs on the mantelpiece. This time Margot sat bolt upright, the spike of her hair becoming just that bit sharper.

"OK, OK, turn it off! I don't know what's going on but just turn it off!"

The huge hand of Robbie Baker, road manager, consultant, arranger of things, wheeler and dealer, reached out to the tape deck and ejected the cassette.

"And that," he said, placing the tape on the coffee-table next to the player, "is only after playing eight seconds of the recording."

He beamed a smile of victory.

She narrowed her eyes in return.

"That's an untouched tape, an actual recording of one of their gigs?"

He nodded.

"And that's The Reflex playing, the night they won the competition?"

Robbie Baker's grin widened as he raised one eyebrow.

"That's right. You've got it, from the horse's mouth. Me. You can have the exclusive inside story for the agreed amount of dosh, subject of course to the usual conditions: in particular, that you don't reveal your source. I want to go on working for these guys, they're going to be very big business."

Margot reached into her shoulder bag and pulled out a small clear plastic box marked *Property of Yoof Edge*. With a snug "click" she fitted the cassette into the recorder.

"OK, Robbie, I want my money's worth so I'll get straight to the point. I'll be frank, no bull – to most of us in this business The Reflex are rubbish. They play nerd music; they're puerile trashcan fodder. Just another grotty collection of acne-ridden teenagers, trying to be cooler than a polar bear's freezer. Yet, late last year, they turned the music industry on its head, winning the London finals for best live band. Now according to another reviewer on our paper, the recent Club Excellent gig was just heaving with bodies. It was outrageous, it was zippy, it was ... well, it was *weird*. I mean – why such enthusiasm for such utter dross? Tell me, babe, tell it like it was." She thought for a moment. "Perhaps that's 'is', tell me like it *is*."

She pressed the record button.

The big man nodded. He was going to have to be up front with a reporter like Margot LaStrange, any bull and he wouldn't get paid.

"This isn't an easy story to tell, and it's going to take some believing. I'm not even sure where to begin."

Margot LaStrange melted back into the sofa and folded her arms. Her special turquoise-blue tinted contact lenses flashed. "From the beginning now, I want to know *everything*."

"I guess it all started when they decided to chuck in music and call it a day. I was at school with them. That's how I got to work for them, if the truth be told; I was going out with Suzie, their lead vocalist – had been for months. We're not together any more, that's why I don't mind telling you all of this.

"The Ramsay Street High School Raw Edge Disco was the turning point. They were all in the sixth form. They weren't known as The Reflex then. They used to call themselves The Buzz Bombs! Can you believe that? The Buzz Bombs! It was the usual teen music group, you know, just doing cover versions of chart stuff, some re-mixes – sampling. There were a few numbers that they tried to write themselves; dreadfully performed but played, in their case, with top quality gear. That made it even more horrendous. Believe me, there's nothing worse than badly played music coming at you with crystal clarity. That was because of Sidney. Sidney and his step-dad, Gross Pockets.

Buying the kid off again, getting the group all the finest stuff. Didn't make no difference, though. Bad is bad; the better you can hear a fumbled guitar chord, the worse it sounds. Get me?

"The band had to finish their final set three numbers early on that night. They had no choice in the matter. The fourth can of Coke had already hit the stage. Most of the buffet had been pasted all over the walls. It had all gone wrong, their playing was *the* pits.

"They left by the back door. Suzie was particularly upset. There'd been tension in the band all week. Kevin, he was the drummer, had been trying to talk everyone round to rehearsing some sort of stage act. He arranges most of their special effects these days. He wanted Suzie to pretend to bite the head off a chicken at the end of the first set. She had got really mad, told him not to be so disgusting and where were they going to get a chicken at that time of night anyhow? But nothing was ever too wild for Kevin, and the band was known for the occasional crazy thing, like the night they let fifty live frogs loose at the College Dance during their number 'Life is a Pond'.

"Kevin loved his gimmicks, which was probably why they let Sid join the band in the first place. I'll let you into a secret though: Sidney never could play. Flashy electronics and Gross Pocket's money, that was Sidney's secret. Kevin liked the gimmick, with the really flashy synthesizer, I mean; getting Sid to join was group insurance for all the gear. Sidney's new dad wanted to make sure that it was nothing but the best for our Sidney, and Kevin knew it!

"Sidney was mortified, poor kid. He hadn't been with the band very long and to be booed off stage in front of your aunties and uncles was really humiliating. Oh, I hadn't told you about that. Gross Pockets had ordered Uncle Frank and Auntie Jean over especially from Northampton. 'Leader of the group is young Sid' and all that, he'd told them.

"The Buzz Bombs were finished but the kids were still good friends. Shared school work, went to the pictures together, messed around and that kind of thing. Suzie and some of the others accepted the truth: they were bad with a capital B. Not just in need of a little practice, but simply hopeless. A few of them still hoped that they might get back together again. Mickey, in particular. Sidney still hung around with them. He was gangly and awkward, he didn't seem to have many friends and I guess they felt sorry for him. They're a good bunch, you know, they stick together and help one another. The break-up hit Sidney hardest, especially after he dyed a little front quiff of his hair with his mother's peroxide. It was his sort of badge for the band, his official rock musician emblem, made him look like a really hip badger – but now he had no band!

"As things turned out it was just as well that they kept with him because that was how we met his cousin William. Yeah, that's right. Bill Foley, as you know him, the mysterious fifth member of the band. The man in the shadows. The electronics genius. He wore thick, pebble glasses then, and he was all skin and bone. He's taken up body-building since and, of course, he's had his nose altered and wears all those designer clothes.

"The first time I saw Bill, it was my last term at school. I saw some of the ex-band members at the school gate talking to this thin, spidery bloke with bottle-bottom specs, held together with a huge wodge of Sellotape. His nose was something else, a weasel would have been envious. His hair was thin and lank, it flopped down on to his head as if it were too tired to do anything else.

"Sidney was there and introduced me to Cousin William. William was, and I quote, 'Jolly pleased to meet me'. Real Hoorah Henry of the first order, a total wally, but it really wasn't the kid's fault, he had *real* problems at home. His parents just pulled him apart. His mother was some sort of doctor, an expert on nerves, muscles, that sort of thing, and his old man was an electronics head who invented things. Sidney told me that they were in competition with one another. Who attended the most conferences, travelled most, published most, fiddled their expenses best – that kind of thing. Each wanted William to follow in their respective footsteps. So William was often off-loaded on to other members of the family one moment, and then pressurized to become an instant genius in nerve-ends or wires and transistors the next. He was now staying with Sidney. Sidney's step-dad had been telling the usual whoppers about how Sidney was a big star in his own band etc. *His* band, I tell you!

"Well, along comes the cousin, sees Sidney's back bedroom full of amplifiers, synthesizers and all that, and assumes that all is hunky-dory. Sidney had lost his bottle with regard to telling the truth about the band – that they had broken up and all that. Of course, William wanted to meet the rest of the gang as soon as possible. They were all very good about it. Suzie realized fairly quickly what was going on and the whole thing was carried off with true tact. What they didn't know was that crafty Kevin saw it all as an opportunity to have another go at re-forming the band.

"Well, what could they do? They didn't want to let Sidney down, make him look stupid, so they just went along with it for a while. Kevin didn't let up. As far as he was concerned they were going to re-form and that was that.

"Then he saw *the* famous advertisement in the local paper. The competition run by Sound Demon FM for the best live band.

"Well, you know what the rules were. Gimmicky, I suppose, but interesting, give them that. The competition was to be Democracy in Action. The local councillors were very hot about that, all lefty political correctness till it hurt. You know, *ta ra ta ra* – let *the people* decide: so the winner would be chosen by the audience. The object of the competition was to find the greatest dance band in London, the one which could best get the whole place bouncing, heaving and shaking. A team of judges would decide by observation which band got the best response. They had a sort of clapometer, but – hey! – forget the usual applause. Show your vote by some real enthusiastic hard get-down-and-give-it-some. Great idea really, clever.

"Kevin had decided that they should enter; it would get the band back together and there was the possibility of a recording contract and the usual degree of fame for the winners. The other kids just wanted to forget it. Suzie felt that enough was enough, but Kevin cut out the ad and passed it on to Sidney before you could say 'fabuloso'.

"Now, stay with this. Kevin decides to go over to see Sidney personally, he thinks that if he can get through to Sidney, then Suzie and the others might follow. Sidney lived on this exclusive estate in Dulwich. His mum and step-dad had this really big garage; in fact, that was where they practised most of the time. It was a little way from the main house, and had all this acoustic insulation. As Kevin walks up the driveway, he hears short bursts of sound from Sidney's synthesizer, followed by the most outrageous laughter. No tune, but with Sid at the keyboard that was nothing unusual. This was different, though. He just heard single notes and the most extraordinary shrieks of laughter. According to Kevin the garage door to the side opened up, and Sidney literally fell out on to the front lawn, rolling on the ground holding his stomach as if he were fit to burst, his legs kicking in the air, tears rolling down his cheeks.

"OK? Now, Kevin goes in, completely bewildered by all of this.

"You need to understand something at this point which I haven't so far mentioned. Cousin William kept hamsters: Sybil and Cynthia. Yeah, you heard me right, hamsters: as in little furry friends with pouches for cheeks. Well, let's face it, everyone needs a pet. They travelled everywhere with him – he adored them and as far as one can tell they kind of liked him, too.

"Sybil and Cynthia were in their cage perched on the top of a trestle-table at the far end of the garage. Beside the cage was a single loudspeaker. William sat behind the synthesizer keyboard with a *very* serious face. Every so often he banged out these single notes. Not playing any particular tune, you understand, just hitting a key and then trying to keep a straight face. Sidney reappeared at the door, pointed at the cage, and then just fell about in another fit of laughter. William readjusted his specs, raised a single fore-finger and with a 5–4–3–2–1 countdown, plunged his finger down on to a deep G bass note. The garage rattled, as did the hamsters' cage, but something was happening inside the hamsters' fun wheel to cause even Wiliam to break out into a grin.

"Think back to what I was telling you about William's parents, what they did for a living, remember that William got hounded by each of them? To please both, our William studied electronics, while taking an interest in his mother's thing with the human nervous system. William may have looked a wally but in fact he was bright. *Very* bright. Every time a certain note was hit on the synthesizer, Sybil and Cynthia would suddenly leap into the air. Sybil was in the fun wheel when Kevin walked in. No note or a B, or a C# or a D and you got a quiet peaceful hamster, nibbling at straw or whatever it is that hamsters nibble. But hit an A G, F, G#, or a certain sequence, and they just went crazy.

"William introduced Sybil and Cynthia as the 'Dancing Rodents' and said that they would win them the competition.

"He had a plan, you see.

"To this day, I don't know what it was that William rigged up. He told Kevin it was based on something his mum called the 'reflex principle'. You know the thing, if you tap just below your knee then your leg jerks upwards – you can't help it, it proves you're alive. Did you ever do that electrical experiment with a dead frog's leg when you were at school? William said that the principle was a piece of cake, something that was 'beneath him', scientifically. He'd rigged up this black box. It went between the synthesizer and the amplifier. Certain notes on the keyboard went through a signal processor change when played. In simple plain English, the sound came out through the speakers and hit you just below the knee like a mild tap on the reflex points. A kind of irritant – William called it 'the tingle'.

"You see, William's hamsters had no choice. They

just had to dance, or let's be precise, to twitch. To move about. It was like scratching an itch, so they did it, and it looked for all the world like dancing!

"William sat Kevin down and carefully explained the principle. At the moment, the signal was at a very low pitch. A bit more work on the black box and what worked for little hamsters would work for us, or ... *an audience.*

"The rest is history, really. They brought William into the group, that was unanimous. I became their roadie and Sidney's step-dad entered them for the competition. There was no problem about it, as long as he could invite the entire family.

"That night was unbelievable. The Club Excellent simply throbbed with the beat. The music was atrocious, OK, I admit it. They still couldn't play any better, but what did that matter? The atmosphere was wild! They opened up with 'Hamster Shuffle'; that's their new single by the way, dedicated to Sybil and Cynthia. Everybody was out there on that dance floor. Twisting, gyrating, twirling. Even the panel of judges. They just couldn't help themselves. The band members had special ear plugs so that the effect was reduced for them, but Sidney chose not to wear them – that's why he's got such a reputation for being so wild. Of course, they cleaned up. They won hands down!

"That's it. Great story, eh?

"Can I have the money now, please?"

There was a thick, fat silence.

Margot LaStrange stared at Robbie. He hadn't noticed that she had switched the tape off long before he had finished the story. Her panda eyes had changed to an angry red.

"If you think that this is some kind of joke, then. . ."

"Every word is true, honestly!" pleaded Robbie.

For a moment she was speechless. Then she quickly gathered up her tapes and hurried towards the door. Her time had been wasted. Taken for a fool with an outrageous bundle of lies and fantasy. She stood in the doorway for a second.

"Don't ask for the rest of the fee. Just *don't* ask! You must have thought I was born yesterday!"

Then she was gone.

The police officer that stopped the bright red Renault on Chelsea Bridge had to help the young blonde girl from her driver's seat. It wasn't that she was hysterical exactly, she was just laughing and mumbling something like "perhaps it was all true".

She was clutching a tape in her right hand.

The policeman explained that he had had to stop her. She was driving all over the place and he was worried that she might be having some kind of seizure. In fact, the car had appeared to dance all the way down Queenstown Road and had almost caused a serious accident at the roundabout.

She muttered something about having put the wrong tape in the car stereo, saying that it didn't belong to her, that she had taken it by mistake and that it wasn't her fault. Her legs just wouldn't keep still. Even the wheels of the car had taken on a life of their own, or so it had seemed.

The policeman eased the cassette out of her hand. It had a white label: THE REFLEX AT CLUB EXCELLENT. Even he had heard of this band. His daughter talked about them all the time, she loved to dance to them, just couldn't help herself. She said the music gave her a special kind of tingle.

The car radio suddenly fizzled into life.

At Radio Sounds FM, the top DJ, Dave Godwin, was about to place The Reflex's latest single on the turntable: 'Hamster Shuffle'. An exclusive first for the station.

In the busy London street the sound of the DJ's voice bounced out through the car windows; everyone seemed to have tuned in to the station.

"OK folks, get on your fun wheels and *dance!*"

Every car radio tuned into the station was about to receive it.

Every car radio.

The music began.

Suddenly, back on the bridge came the unmistakable sound of the crunch of steel on steel and the smashing of glass.

Wicked Disk

Mid-morning has crept up on Kevin Drood, almost unnoticed. The day arrives with a tell-tale shaft of light, a cruel bright blade that pierces the gap in the curtains. The makeshift drapes, rummaged from the housing-estate skips, allow peppered points of daylight to cast a ray of stars across the place where he lies. He is huddled, ungainly, like a broken mannequin.

Kevin opens a single eye, slowly, cautiously. Sticky eyelashes blur his view of the room as he peers over the frayed edge of the tattered eiderdown. He pauses for a moment, uncertain if he has awoken, wondering if perhaps he still dreams. His hand emerges from beneath the cover, which smells of something sweet and sickly, like bad yeast. Outstretched searching fingers fumble for his spectacles.

He coughs and almost gags from the stench of the air. For a moment his hand crawls across the surface of the chair, like a pale-coloured spider, then the tips of his fingers discover something wiry surrounding two thick, smooth circular wedges.

He pulls his spectacles towards him and winds the hooks of the wire arms around his ears; greasy knots of hair become fastened to the sides of his face. The cold metal almost holds his features, as though steel fingers were trying to bring him round, to hold his head steady so that he might recall where he is.

But now, he knows exactly where he is. Exactly.

Another day in the pit of technological revenge for the misunderstood genius.

He groans. His voice almost touches bottom.

Each new day is always unkind. It brings the usual vermin: the kids downstairs in the estate courtyard; milkmen clattering bottles and crates, whilst eyeing shifty-looking tenants half-hidden in doorways. Sometimes the milkmen's tuneless whistling stops whilst an overdue bill is paid. It is a terrible place. But he will never return to his parents; they had never understood him.

Babies squawk. Dogs howl. Eventually, it will become a cacophony: a symphony of blaring radios that will crowd the air with rubber-band music. On the floor above, the washing machine that never rests will rattle and shake his ceiling.

For a moment he clenches his teeth, remembering the past week. There had been the doorstep callers to contend with. Young children often knocked, daring one another to stand their ground the longest, before he opened up. Usually they would run away with shrieks of terrible laughter, knowing that he wouldn't dare leave his doorway to give chase.

Recently, another kind of caller had troubled him: the savers of souls, drawn to the estate's hive of decaying humanity like flies to meat.

There were many who needed saving here.

Perhaps it was something to do with the challenge? Was that why they came?

The Sally Army Band came first, risking a half-hour in the yard last Saturday with their clapped out brass and broken tambourines. Roaming groups of Jehovah's Witnesses followed. They had knocked repeatedly at his door, asking whether he had found the way, the truth and the light. They called when he had finally managed to doze off, or late when he was beginning to get into a computer game or write a new virus.

There were others, too, all wishing to take you away to paradise.

Kevin's knuckles still sting, grazed and sore from a recent doorstep encounter. The pain reminds him yet again that he is alive; feeling returns in increments, slowly searing his body with a poker heat. His mouth is a thick mass of puffy gum, swollen and full. He groans. The abscess that throbs hot beneath his tooth hasn't healed; it is as raw and infected as everything else around him.

How he hates the world.

For a moment he considers whether to put his head back beneath the cover and to drown out the day. It would be easy. Kevin is a night creature, and for that, the pit suits. Spurned by the day, he has long grown used to the dark, rejecting the cruelty of sunlight. But there is something he must do. He remembers with a small, monkey-grin, that he has to listen to the news again this morning.

Throwing the cover to one side, he swings his spindly legs round to sit on the edge of the couch. A fluttering feeling inside his head, like the flurry of a captured moth, makes him feel dizzy and there is a pain across his eyes. He had fallen asleep around the middle of the night. He glances at the radio and discovers that he just has time to gather his thoughts.

This morning the room looks worse than usual. The brightness of daytime somehow shows too much, revealing his secrets: piles of dirt and dust; magazines strewn across the floor; cardboard boxes of second-hand paperbacks stacked against stained, peeling wallpaper.

The day corrupts his pleasures, too. It casts a reflected glare across his computer screen, tainting and obscuring, casting a dust-grey sheen. Spoiling.

In the cloak of night, alone and undisturbed, he can melt into the world of programmed dreams and imagine impossible worlds, live unimaginable lives. Fight and quest with dragons and demons, hide away from the drum of reality in his adult fairyland, surf the Internet and, of course, plot new ways of revenge. He has his mission.

Kevin currently has another burden to bear; there has been little time for game-playing these last nights. He has spent acres of time swapping cables, disks and disk-drives in the hope that perhaps the problem was a simple software fault, unlikely as that might be. Then he re-copies and edits disks in a frenzy until, feeling sick and confused, he can take no more.

It has been the same every night, all week. He lifts his body and slouches into the chair that faces his screen. A mass of wire feels soft around his feet like loops of snakes. A jumble of disks that he had swept off his plywood desk in a sudden surge of explosive frustration lie scattered across the wires.

He moans, realizing that the fault is still with him, and pushes his lank, unwashed hair back from his face. He stares towards the screen, a knot tightens inside and he grinds his teeth like a coffee mill on stubborn beans. The screen is as he left it, locked in a reverse video with that awful shining face grinning out from the centre of a jumble of text. It mocks him, taunting with the usual expression: a hideous clown face, frozen into a laugh. There is that awful American message, too: 'Have a nice day.'

He wipes his forearm across his face. There is a frightening justice here that confounds him. It sits uncomfortably inside his conscience like a stone. After all, is it not Kevin that writes programs to cause chaos? Is it not his genius that destroys and eradicates?

Now, at last, his own system has fallen foul of someone else's trick: a victim of the Mirror Clown Virus.

It's a work of brilliance. He has to admit that part of him is fascinated, mesmerized by its ingenuity whilst being puzzled how it has entered his computer system. He's heard the rumours. That it's mean and can corrupt everything.

The first and most startling thing that it did was to turn the screen into a silver sheet, like the dead scales of a landed fish. His first encounter scared him to death. It was late. One minute he was devising a way to get out of the Castle of Dromeda from the third level, and the next he was staring at his shadowed jowls; pin-prick eyes intense and set like an animal's.

He next encountered it when the text of another adventure game was turned on its head in seconds, simply by swapping the words for their antonyms: *good* to *bad*, *full* to *empty*, *open* to *shut*. It even worked on images and numbers: a negative number to a positive, and, of course, that made garbage of number-crunching.

He cries out suddenly as the clock radio breaks the silence. But this is what he has woken for.

Local news dribbles its way through mundane items. He listens carefully – there has to be *something*. A young girl's emotionless voice announces that, "the mysterious computer virus that has hit the city has now contaminated the hospital mainframe computer during the night, causing havoc. One patient undergoing computer-monitored surgery is in a serious condition." Kevin smiles as he listens to the whining of the hospital administrator as he is interviewed. It is the same little shit that lost him his porter's job when he worked there after leaving school, and now *he* is in trouble. Kevin's virus is spreading quicker and better than he had ever dreamed it would. A program that scrambles *everything*.

48

He turns to his monitor.

The stare of the clown face dampens his good feeling.

He reaches out his hand and searches for the off switch. The room plunges into the more natural gloom of curtained daylight as the afterglow of the screen dies.

Feeling restless, Kevin stares at his mail for several minutes. The black coffee which he was sipping has gone cold. He knows what is in the envelopes. There are envelopes addressed to previous different "tenants", the council never check up. There is the usual crop of red reminders of unpaid bills, a renewal subscription to a computer games magazine, *Orange Dwarf*, and a long, grey envelope with the words CompuRead Ltd in the top left-hand corner. This envelope he places against a china lamp. They are good payers and the money is running out from the last contract he'd taken; he might value another "one-off" from that company. It pays for his mission in life.

His other items consist of junk mail and a stiff card envelope, post-marked Columbia, USA. This will be more goodies: pirate stuff from his American contact.

This morning the envelopes feel sticky between his fingers and he half wonders if they shouldn't go straight into the bin. Could he really be experiencing guilt? Could something from the spate of God Squad callers be rubbing off on him?

Kevin replaces his mug on a side table for a

moment and, yet again, thinks deeply about the mirror virus. Had it come from any of the programs Jim had sent him? Not intentionally, surely? After all, they'd exchanged things for years now.

"No," he mutters, "not Jim Schneider. Not knowingly. He warns me of problems, he doesn't send them."

"Darn virus," he mumbles as he falls back in his seat, allowing the remaining envelopes to drop to the floor.

He feels tired, washed out and lower than he's felt in weeks. The virus has deprived him of his toy and made restless days worse. It fills his thoughts — angering and frustrating him. A sick feeling inside contains the fear that he might have to junk every programme he's lovingly stolen.

As he stretches his head back and yawns, he reaches out and switches off the radio. Suddenly, a sharp rap on the front door disturbs the drum of stillness.

Little kids? he thinks. *No, not kids, not so early. I'll give them a good kicking if. . .*

He perches himself on the edge of his chair and gazes into space. What should his next move be? His chin rests in his hands.

The knock returns. Unusual.

Perhaps not kids after all, he considers. *Not knocking twice, so soon*.

He stretches himself out of his chair and shuffles towards the curtains. He peers through the gap. At first he thinks it is the police. Several dark figures stand there, all dressed in a similar uniform style: navy blue or black. Then he realizes that there are two children as well, a boy and a girl.

He pulls his face away from the chink. Kevin cannot understand what he has seen. After a moment the knock returns, a third time. He leans forward to take another, longer, look.

His adult visitors are tall; there is something about them, too, a distinguished air maybe? Both are elderly men, with large black books tucked beneath their arms. Their skin looks smoother than marble despite their age. Each rests a hand on the shoulder of the boy and the girl who stand, almost ceremoniously, before them. The detail of their dress is clearer now: each wears a thick cloth, so heavy with loops and folds it looks like a cape, with large brimmed circular hats pulled firmly down on to their heads.

"Oh, no!" he cries. "Not another religous group! Who are these then, Mormons?"

Kevin allows a grin to stretch his face; he can hardly believe it.

"Mormons, on Stockwell Park Estate! Witnesses, the Sally Army, Baptists and now Mormons. Lord help them if any of the McHugh kids catch them on the stairways."

As he pulls the curtains shut, another, harder knock rattles the door.

"Let them rot," he says, hauling himself over to the couch.

Another, shorter knock follows, and after that there is silence.

Kevin dreams of laughing clown masks that hide his anxious face, and of mirrors that ripple like shining, watery pools. Suddenly, the dream dissolves into an aerial view of his computer screen. A knocking, far-off at first, moves closer. It is a persistent rapping; it now comes from the disk-drive and is urgent as if somebody or something wants to get out.

He sits upright, awakening with a start; a trickle of sweat runs down his face and his gums hurt more than ever.

The knocking continues. It takes only seconds for his roving eyes to settle, and for him to realize that the noise is coming from out in the passageway.

"I don't believe it," he says.

Kevin does not know why, but he adjusts his spectacles and gets up off the couch. He scratches his backside and proceeds to the front door, not bothering to check who might be there. He believes he knows who it is, and he is angry.

Without engaging the security chain, usually an automatic move, he opens the door and looks out into the day. The brightness stings his eyes at first; he might be staring into a furnace. The quartet he had spied through his curtains earlier stand again before him. Black wedge shapes peek out from beneath the folds of neat and sombre dress.

"Good day, neighbour," smiles the man to his right,

with a polite bow. His companion, an older man with a white pencil-thin moustache, touches the brim of his hat. The children remain silent; their wide eyes stare upwards with serious angel-like expressions.

Kevin stares back.

"I don't understand this," he whispers to himself. "What . . . just what am I doing here on the doorstep?"

"We have come to tell you of the Coming of the Kingdom, neighbour, of the news that those who open their hearts may receive healing through the power of. . ."

"Wait, wait, just wait a minute. . ." Kevin tries to collect himself, waving his hand meaninglessly.

"Neighbour?" enquires the older man, frowning.

Kevin stops waving; talking isn't helping his abscess.

"You ain't my neighbour. My neighbour's a sixteen stone black guy with a wife who's left him with a bunch of children." Then he adds, with uncharacteristic pleasantness, "I . . . I work nights, you've got me at a bad time . . . and I can't. . ." He takes a deep breath, wondering why he is bothering with an explanation.

"We understand. We'll call back, we know you are in need."

Need, he thinks. "Need? No. No, I'm not religious and I don't follow the Mormon preaching and. . ."

"Mormon?" asks the small boy, with an uncomprehending gaze.

The group laugh. Even the little girl manages a smile as she turns towards the boy, making a gesture suggesting they might share a secret.

"We are not Mormon, neighbour, oh no. We are messengers, healers."

"What is your work?" asks the older man.

"Computers, and..." He could have bitten his tongue; he realizes that he is walking into their gambit, actually talking, exchanging with them. "Look. I have to get back to bed and catch up on a heavy night. I'm not interested, anyway."

The older man removes the black book from beneath his arm and holds it out like a gift.

"The Word, neighbour. The Book. The Method. In faith, you see? Just take it and read, then perhaps we might call back on a more opportune occasion when..."

Something tightens like piano wire inside Kevin. His irritability shifts within him like coarse sand.

"I'm going. I don't read. Just..."

"We have all kinds of media, sir," says the little boy. "Video. Perhaps you have a machine? Or maybe a talking cassette will be easier if you cannot read?"

"Of course I can read, you little..."

"We are aware of the twentieth-century, neighbour," says the older man in a gentle but firmer voice.

"We even provide a way for you," smiles the little girl, holding out a black envelope. She turns to the boy. "Our neighbour said he works with computers – let us give him the disk."

For a reason Kevin cannot fully understand, something makes him recoil. He shrinks with fear or loathing, he is uncertain which. He steps back, allowing the door to swing fully open as he does so.

All four of his visitors are smiling now, their heads tilted to one side, eyes hard as marble orbs in Grecian statues. Their faces are powder white, reminding him of the Mirror Clown. The sunlight etches their outline, which is now filled with solid shadow. They are becoming a mysterious blackness. For a few seconds he feels the skin on the nape of his neck prickle and crawl. He can stand it no longer.

"I feel dizzy..."

"Oh?" says the girl. "Do you need healing?"

He slams the door hard with a sudden urgency, surprised at his breathlessness.

Quickly returning to his room, he curls into a ball beneath the quilt cover and sucks at his thumb.

Kevin starts back at the computer later than usual. The night has brought dreams of solutions to his problems, of vaccine disks that will protect and eradicate the menace that has dropped into his life. He decides to try to save what he can from the hard disk and maybe reformat it. He wonders if the virus had been lurking within the machine before he got it.

Kevin runs his fingers across an unopened software package and decides to try something new first. The game that he opens is, of course, a pirated copy, recently acquired.

The screen starts up as usual. Everything is as it should be. Perhaps it is too normal.

He loads "The Valley of Mists".

The drive purrs softly.

At the C> prompt he types MISTS.

A purr accompanies twisting fog, which stretches across the screen.

Good graphics, he thinks, as the grey weaves a series of shades, promising special adventures.

The sudden rap on the front door makes him catch his breath. He is very nervous today.

"Damn!" he spits.

The knocking returns, harder, longer and much more persistent this time.

Kevin pushes his chair back.

The door will burst.

"I'm coming!" he yells.

He pauses on his way to the front door, and decides to check through the window. Crossing to the curtains, he peers out. Evening is settling in, but a single paint-spattered bulb on the balcony casts light across a dark outline. A huddled figure stands beside his front door, like a dark elf. At first he is uncertain who or what the visitor can be.

He pulls his head back.

"They're back! They're back, the creeps! I don't believe it."

His face feels flush and full as, with wide strides, he continues to the hallway and unhooks the security chain. He holds the door wide.

"Sling it!" he screams, and then finds himself gawping downwards.

He had expected the entire quartet, but here instead is the little girl, alone. The girl is smiling again; she searches out his eyes.

The next few moments are blurred. A soft beating, like the blow from the wings of a huge bird, fills the space behind his eyes, each blow tilts his view of the world. The girl stretches out her hand, he isn't sure why. Her voice sounds slow and slurred.

"Take it, please. *It's wicked.*"

He registers the movement as an act of aggression. Surely all that she is doing is offering him something, a book maybe? Already the door is swinging shut from the full weight of his push, and still the girl's arm is outstretched towards him.

The black sleeve jams in the opening. Kevin panics as the door swings back. As the sleeve withdraws, the latch clicks and the door shuts on the tips of tiny fingers.

A terrible scream rents the air, as something red and wet trickles down the door-jamb.

Kevin falls back against the door, his breath coming fast, the cries continue outside. A black kite shape flutters down by his feet.

The girl's cries are frightening. He lifts his hands to his ears and tries to drown out her voice.

"Invasion!" he cries. "Invasion of privacy! It was an accident and it's your own fault!"

He runs from the hallway and back to the living-room.

The computer screen has already turned to a perfect mirror, bouncing back and reversing everything that it sees. He lowers his face to the monitor and stares long and hard as muddled voices outside come and go. He half expects to hear a knock, for footsteps to return, but instead the sounds of crying and comforting whispers disappear with slow footsteps, down towards the stairway. They have gone without complaint.

He continues to stare at his reflection. He cannot see his eyes, there are only dark spaces set in a paste face.

Suddenly the mirror screen shatters like a crazed windscreen and the laughing clown face pushes through, grinning back at him.

"Have a nice day."

He whimpers like a whipped dog.

An amusement arcade laugh fills the room.

Kevin listens by the window, resisting the temptation to peek outside, but he listens for any tell-tale footsteps, any snatches of muffled conversation which might announce the police or the return of his callers. But there are none.

The night is uncommonly quiet.

Feeling braver, he goes to the front door, unable to recall whether he had replaced the security chain. He hadn't.

He stops for a moment and listens carefully. He is vaguely aware of stepping on something soft like a sheet of paper. He crouches down and notices a black envelope. Something pale that oozes a dark coloured softness spoils the edge of it.

Isn't there a piece of tiny fingernail there, too?

Not wanting to consider this further he brushes it off against the doormat and rises with the envelope in his hand. The unsealed flap is tucked within the body of the envelope. Creasing the opening reveals a computer disk. There is nothing else inside and a quick inspection reveals that there is no writing or printing of any kind anywhere on the disk.

He returns in a drunken walk to the living-room. The computer is switched off.

"New disk," he mumbles. "I bet it's a Bible tutor, or a publicity disk of some kind. Who did they say they were?"

He thinks for a moment, recalling the words.

"We are not Mormon, neighbour, we are messengers..."

A nagging feeling inside begins to irritate him. A curiosity he finds hard to resist surges through his thoughts. It will not go away.

"Why not?" he sighs.

Switching the computer on, he waits whilst the operating system purrs.

"Keep off my back, Coco," he hisses, between clenched teeth.

Kevin hesitates, but then slips the disk into his disk-drive, snapping the gate lever shut with a flick of his finger.

At the screen prompt he types A:Dir to show him a list of files on the disk.

Three file names flash up:

The Word.Exe.

Faith.Syst.

Healing.Exe.

Kevin considers these for a moment and types: The Word.

The screen goes black, there is a soft tinkling sound, like winter crystal.

It brings peace, calming him somehow. His command has worked, a message spreads across the centre of the screen:

"Shall ye enter the gates?"

Kevin frowns. He presses ENTER.

The same message returns.

"You're not thinking, Kevin," he murmurs. "It's asking you a question."

He types Y for Yes, to accept.

The fairy notes float out on to his desk as the program runs.

"He sent forth his word, and healed them, and delivered them from destruction."

Kevin's eyes widen.

"We are messengers. Healers."

Now he remembers. There was something about the file name, too. He presses ENTER.

"Are any sick among you?" appears on the screen.

Kevin types Y.

For a moment a brown wash of light flickers about him. The twinkle of the disk returns, but this time, it is different. It is sweeter, more musical, like wind-chimes.

His fingers freeze, poised above the keys. The screen goes black again, and the corner lamp goes off. The room becomes a sticky darkness.

The black that fills his vision is far too black, as though shutters have dropped down from beneath his heavy eyelids. The effect lasts moments only.

Kevin gradually becomes aware of a shuddering, a low rumble as if a spring was bubbling beneath the floor; it seems to echo in the flat below. The notion of a burst pipe flashes across his mind, but these sounds are natural, organic. Quickly the rumbling changes to an urgent rush, like a far-off avalanche.

The screen flashes white.

Poker-white. Molten-white, like the heart of a furnace.

Kevin tries to push himself away from the desk, but as he drops his hands across the keyboard he realizes that his fingertips have become fastened to the keys. Suddenly, he finds that he is typing in code, leaving red prints on the keys as he taps.

Shafts of brightness, sharp as lasers cut around the edges of the keys. They shine up from the keyboard and into his face. His mouth falls limply open; he is unable to help himself. A great wind rushes around him. He tries to turn his gaze away from the screen, but it is impossible.

Something is coming. From out of the light.

Angel voices fill the room as a slender-fingered hand reaches out towards him. He catches sight of the edge of a robe and as the hand gently turns, he sees something within the palm – a mark.

"My God. . ." he whispers. "What graphics!"

"Thou dost show me the path," flashes at him from deep within the screen.

Kevin's hands feel hot and the cavern of his mouth, now filled with light, tastes sweet.

The word *"Christ"*, ripples into view.

"What graphics!" he whispers again, as the light fills his mind. "She was right, *it is wicked*!"

Several hours later, Kevin sits before the computer again. The strange disk is set within the drive, ready to go.

His hands are cooler now, but still he holds them before his face in amazement. The grazes from last week's doorstep encounter have completely healed. He feels better in himself, better than he has felt for months, maybe even years. His mouth is fresh and clean, not stale and sour. There is no longer the taste of abscess.

Quickly, he executes the loading tasks, eager to see what will happen. So far the Mirror virus has failed to click in. If the program can heal his mouth, perhaps it will heal his computer. As before, the files flash across the screen and he loads The Word.

The message, *"Shall ye enter the gates?"* drops into view.

Kevin presses the Y key.

The tinkling resumes.

He watches and waits, his tongue lolling from the side of his mouth like a panting dog.

The sound from the drive stops.

An aching silence follows.

"Come on, come on," he murmurs.

The screen pixels appear to flex threateningly, to crumple like metallic foil.

No, he thinks, *not the Clown virus – just let me load the program*.

A message ripples across.

"He sent forth his word, and healed them, and delivered them from destruction."

He presses the ENTER key and holds his breath.

After a moment, he is asked the question: "Are any sick among you?"

He types Y and raps out a wild card path, to examine all the files on the hard disk and to run a system check.

The music-box chime returns.

Kevin's fingers grip the sides of the desk. He leans forward, hungry to know more, getting so close to the screen that he can smell the heat of it.

The screen turns black and the room falls into darkness. He waits as if beneath an eclipse. This time he can feel the blackness. Taste it on his lips, sense its pressure.

As before there is a rumbling, a far-off crackle of thunder. The patter of scurrying rats flutters around the edges of his room, behind the skirting. He feels the floor move, just a fraction, as if the concrete that divides the flats might be cracking.

Does he hear a sound over his shoulder? Ancient,

rusting hinges creak wide somewhere in the gloom behind him.

The computer screen melts into space; the surface is barely visible. Red shimmering letters cross before him – floating there, turning his face the colour of glowing coals.

"Him that stole, steal no more.

"Do no more harm to any man."

Kevin pulls back.

The message appears to drip and pool like a wet paint daub, but perhaps it is not paint?

The message changes to another.

"Welcome to the kingdom."

The crunch of broken glass seems to echo around the place where he sits. He hears a low growl.

"Thou dost show me the path," flashes up on the screen.

Kevin swallows. He feels icy sweat trickle down his back. A silvery glow, like the beam of a flashlight, creeps in from the corners of the monitor.

He freezes with fear. The Mirror virus is coming.

More crunching glass sounds cut into the murmur of the room. This time a harsh grating surges from inside the computer. It is as if metal were being twisted.

The empty gate of disk-drive B spits a fine blade edge of orange out from its slot.

Kevin's jaw slackens. The air smells bad and hot, not bright and clear as before.

The light on the screen grows and the message

dissolves, reforming into other words. The word *"show"* dissolves into *"hide"*.

"Thou dost hide the path from me."

The Mirror virus is almost there, reversing everything bit by bit.

The noise of laughter explodes inside his head, as he reaches out a trembling hand. He struggles to find the switch.

The new message, the entry to the program, shines just as before: *"Christ"*.

A dull thud sounds within the darkness, as though something has fallen to the floor behind him from a great height. The moment freezes time. There is something waiting at the disk-drive gate. At first Kevin thinks that the disk has ejected. He looks down.

The thing that shoots out at him is not a disk. It comes from Hell's letter-box. He stares in horror as a tangle of cables rush towards him and rip through his shirt.

But they aren't cables.

They are an unholy mixture of sinew and bone and claw.

A searching, anxious, pointed nail draws a line in blood across his chest, marking out the spot where his heart thuds. He screams with the music of demented laughter.

The prefix *"Anti-"* has dropped into place before the word *"Christ"*. He watches in horror as the word *"holy"* dissolves into *"unholy"* at the top of the screen.

A great wash of colour, like shimmering red silk,

gushes generously on to the keyboard. The screen reflects the agony of realization just before the familiar smiling face of Coco the Clown fills the monitor frame, having successfully corrupted another programme. The computer crashes.

The clock radio fizzes into life. The glow from the digital letters picks out his twitching, huddled body, which is spread across the desk.

"Have a nice day."

Jimi's Axe

For Jeff Beck – thanks, Jeff!

There was a gang of us and we all went back some time together, but Machine-Head and Soho Lil went back a long way. They played in a band together. You know the kind of thing, it's in the archives. Some reworked videos of *Top of The Pops* (as they called the show) – they demonstrate how they used to do it. I mean, Machine-Head actually played with his fingers – he made sounds for real on a musical instrument and Lil sang alone, no computer-aid! Try that today! Let's face it, today's kids wouldn't know what you were doing or what you were talking about!

Lil had gone over to agency work. OK, fair enough, a lot of old-timers have to find new ways of making a living, but I'd also heard that she hated it and had been experimenting lately. Auditioning machines bored her, even those with a high G in Steinberg Artificial Intelligence. But to Lil, a machine was a machine. That was Lil for you; despite her own replacement parts she *did* like real flesh.

I was fifteen and had a part-time job in the holidays working for a music publishers. The word was out that Lil had devised something special for the Londonhosted Eurovision Song Contest. A new kind of entry, a song which linked computer-aid with flesh and bone. The concept was the talk of the business, I soon learned. Hardware engineers everywhere trembled.

The Eurovision officials were dubious at first, but they eventually gave the all-clear; perhaps they wanted a bit of controversy, spice up ticket sales. Recently, there'd been talk on the Cyberspace music magazine, *Melody Designer*, that feeling was coming back into music, and so this would be topical.

I was curious to see what she was up to. We had become friends – I made deliveries to her agency. She said I could drop by and watch the UV implodes being seeded into her two new protogees. These were two young musicians she nicknamed her "Chickadees".

I struggled through the heaped wooden stalls of gizmo gadgetry and techno-toy subways to the narrow alleyway that led to her office. Soho Lil's office was where it had always been: set in London's Brewer Street and spread across the first two floors overlooking the market. All the rooms had been knocked through to recreate the New York loft office, so that there'd be no disorientation for her Chickadees if they travelled there by Lambda Mode – beamed over from the States. Lil had her own personal machine in there.

The agency camera must have caught me as I turned the corner from the market because the main street office door swung open and I heard a heave of thick-breathed purrs and coos: "Dahling, oh dahling, my leetle boyfriend, you know where I am. Are you going to come and visit me?"

The door clicked shut behind me as I entered repro London. I passed a guy on the stairs who looked shifty. He was hidden inside a long, dark raincoat he'd probably got from a stall in the market. The old hang-dog guilt hung all around him like smoke that wouldn't clear.

At the second-floor landing, the pale magnolia paint-blistered decor, which Lil had had specially created from old photos (designer-seediness), suddenly opened into bright-burning neon lights. A blue sign announced "The Lillian Lee Agency".

Halogen nightshade lamps back-lit the walls, attracting the evening moths into the paths of custom-built atmosphere recyclers. The leaves were every-where, their shoots sneaking out of any crevice, nook or cranny they could find. They needed trimming, too.

I peered through the archway.

"Dahling, come in!" came the greeting from the corner shadows.

Lil herself sat behind the huge old Margaret Thatcher Memorial desk which she'd won way back as a gift from the National Lottery. Her fur eye-patch now sported a single bright jewel, but she still wore the same unique, black plastic one-piece which fed most of her remaining vital organs. She was one heck of a fifty per cent android.

Behind her was the photograph. That was a *real* antique. The music-hall comedian with the big beak stared down at her out of the frame. "To Lil, love Jimmy" was scrawled across the bottom of the picture, although of course she couldn't possibly have known him. We all knew she just wrote that on for fun.

Her rich ruby-red lips sucked on a hooker pipe which bubbled contentedly at the edge of her desk. A present given by Machine-Head from way back, it always came out when he visited and he always brought her a bit of hardware to dissolve into the mix. Give Lil her due, she was always in favour of serious fun, in front of visitors, too.

"Hi, Lil!" I kept my distance in case I caught some of her smoke, and had I got any closer she'd have wanted to kiss me on the mouth for sure and that would have been terrible.

"You've come to stare, dahling?"

I grinned and looked about.

"The grape-vine eez so effeeecent. I tell you, my boy, this eez one Eurovision Contest where the audience won't have to just slide those nasty, *nasty* modems into their heads to hear the music. I have two of the best Chickadees here, and they are actually going to override the MBI 0100 computer and thought-play a solo!"

I spun round. "A solo!"

Lil beamed behind a cloud of blue smoke.

"Invention – on the spot. Straight from out of the heads of the dahlings! They will make music – the word now? What eez the word? Improvise."

The two Chickadees that were to front Lil's new

band were sat patiently in iron chairs beside her desk. Their heads had been re-shaved and the younger-looking one had a custom plastic surgery beak-job (in imitation of Lil's pic). He was already having the seed beds surgically implanted by Doc Holland, whom I hadn't seen for goodness knows how long since he'd given up his chiropody practice. The old leather flask was still kept by the laser, as always, so I guessed he was much the same as ever. Lil had even bought him a shake controller.

"Machine-Head eez going to speak to them about music, dahling. That's why he's here! We 'ave a good program to play, if my Chickadees can learn a simple melody and improvise at a pre-programmed point – then..."

"I mean, improvise! Make up music!" I gasped. "For a Euro?"

In the other corner of the room I caught the huge frame and unmistakable ears of Machine-Head. He grunted a greeting at me but didn't turn around. He was surrounded by several other wannabees who Lil had obviously auditioned and rejected. One had had his features altered to look like Cliff Richard. They were waiting to be returned to New York when a Lambda-line came free. I didn't know what was up at first; they all seemed preoccupied, buzzing like bees around a honey pot.

Soho Lil reached out a satin gloved-hand. She was mid-inhalation but I couldn't refuse so I reached over and tugged on one of the flesh-fingers hard and caught her look, straight in the good eye, which didn't look quite so good this evening.

Machine-Head just gurgled and raised his huge hands to the gleaming gold keys which sprouted from his head. He smiled reluctantly, and then opened his mouth as his fingers turned two of the keys simultaneously. The high squeal of an E-sharp harmonized with its bass partner as he greeted me with his four-note calling-card. The room shook as the sound screamed out from the hard "O" of his mouth, grating through the sandpaper and steel filing box of a larynx, the best Doc could do.

One of the wannabees around the table staggered back. Poor dope – he'd never seen anything like it before and obviously thought that Machine-Head's tuners were simply some form of head-gear deco. Of course, they weren't.

Machine-Head had taken the mutation in good spirits, and accepted the price for hanging on with Lil's early implodes for longer than was safe. Another one of Lil's experiments. It was his own fault, but he'd quite got used to being a musical instrument. Lil had Doc make a feature of them and got them gold-plated at her own expense. Lil's good like that.

So, I got greeted with Machine-Head's four-note riff. Some of the Chickadees around the table looked over at me for a second or two, but that was all. Everyone's attention was rooted in the object which lay on the table.

It had been wrapped in some kind of red shawl and there was a black wooden case beneath the table.

I couldn't believe my eyes when I got a real good look at it. I know something about antiques, you see. That was it, that was my moment to see a real "axe".

The customized paint-job was very old now, and flaky, but its character remained. The blond shine seemed just a touch *too* precious. It was like looking at the sun; a golden glow which shimmered and trembled as if it might be the gateway to some powerhouse of energy, almost a nuker's tool-box containing something too awesome and dangerous to unleash.

The ingrained veins of 24-carat were there, too.

I couldn't believe that I was actually looking at one. I'd seen pictures in the old history books and there were one or two in a museum in Memphis, but to actually have the same instrument *just laid out there*! I mean, an instrument that could easily have belonged to one of the first ever stage-stompers!

Despite the ornamental paintwork the unmistakable identity warmed through: a Gibson SG Special, copy. *A real guitar* – can you believe it? An axe – as they used to call it – as used in bygones. The arabic shape: sweeping curves which curled in towards the neck at the dual horns of the body. The tapered, rebated edge was still finely honed, though the years had etched the finish with chips and spots of paint.

There were little brown burns on the top horn, too.

Dual pick-ups lay in the centre of the body. They radiated power from the mirror sheen of 35-carat plate, past the set of original Ike Isaac strings, specially wound. Then the pearl inlaid neck swept up to the jewel of the piece: solid gold, machine head-keys, even brighter than Machine-Head's own, which still cast the reflecting light of the halogens and neon out into a million different directions.

"Eets only a copy, but good, eh?" said Lil.

I nearly said something, but remained silent. Simply staring at the shape was enough.

Machine-Head re-folded the red velvet shawl around the guitar with the reverence of religious ceremony. His huge hands smoothed the cloth along the neck and then with the attitude of a humble bondsman, he lifted the bundle into the air for a moment and then laid it to rest in front of Soho Lil.

"I don't believe it," I whispered.

Lil puffed on her pipe.

I rushed over to the desk and gently pulled the red shawl away. I examined the horns again and then the neck, hoping. I thought I knew where this came from. My eyes grew; I saw them, inlaid with pearl – the special initials just above the third fret: JB.

Soho Lil stopped puffing on the hooker pipe. Her eye burned into me from across the desk.

"I see you notice, eh? JB, dahling. JB."

The lips pouted, teased, tantalized me.

"JB," she repeated.

I couldn't speak for a moment, and then I stuttered the question.

"It belonged to *him*, the legendary JB?"

"Seemed to, dahling, seemed to. I never knew he played with zee copies, though."

She raised the end of the pipe and took in an extra inhalation of some of the hardware treat.

The lips made the initials again. "JB."

I stared across the room to where Doc was just tidying up the seed beds in one of the Chickadees heads. He caught my look and nodded with a prominent puffed-up expression.

"JB," he said.

"Holy Moses," I said, not caring about watching the implode routine any more.

The other Chickadee, who was waiting for seeding, hadn't been allowed to leave his seat. Doc sometimes liked to work in pairs so that he could check the work. Usually the MBI 0100 computer did it all – you just brought in your own software – but if the Chickadees were to interact they had to be wired up in parallel. Doc could be damn good.

"Who was JB?" asked the Chickadee with the beak-job.

I rolled my eyes.

Soho Lil almost choked on her hooker and Machine-Head looked as if he was going to try and crash an entire run of notes out through his mouth. I was glad he didn't. When Head went into notes it was rough.

"We think the axe was his," he said abruptly.

"Axe?" asked one of the Chickadees. "That's, that's what this is?"

"Of course, dahlings," chirped in Lil. "Axe, it eez a geetar. It's old, too. Only a copy, you understand, but what a copy. It belonged to one of the first music hero-Combos, that's what my baby says."

Machine-Head nodded again in agreement. He stroked his grey beard as if it might be a pet dangling there on the edge of his chin. His face was beginning to sadden. It was all that memory, he really was a soft toad.

"JB?" asked the Chickadee with the beak-job.

I couldn't stand it any longer; I had studied it all at school in music history.

"Jimi Beckton," I said. Certain now of my ground. I looked at the neck of the axe again. "It was used by *the* very first Combo before the engineers took over the industry. The player was put together by Astrodomus, if my memory serves me well. Did it in a little high-tech drive-in round the back of Great Newport Street somewhere. The forerunner of today's musicians, but there were no implodes and silicon-injected aesthete. Twenty per cent flesh, but the rest had to be fabricated or replicate. Point was that the musicians actually did perform. I mean, they had to actually play."

The Chickadees round the table were puzzled. It was easy to see why they hadn't got through Lil's audition. They could not understand the concept of playing a musical instrument.

I sighed. Machine-Head was quiet; he was just welling up with nostalgia.

"It wasn't all chip and data like today, they really had to cut it then. The point of the Combo was that they could reproduce some of the best of early music."

"Listen to him, dahlings," purred Lil. She could tell I was enjoying sounding so knowledgeable. "You Chickadees might learn something, put a leetle soul into your programs."

I sighed again. The two Chickadees were leaning forward in their chairs, which annoyed Doc as he was trying to work, but he liked to listen, too. The group round the table just stood quite still.

I was going to have to get basic.

"A Combo was a musician made up of some of the best examples of solid gold genius." I felt like my music teacher. "JB had early music rock guitar hero genes spliced in. They'd been donated to the Musician Union Archive by the performers, so we were OK. Had a bit of nearly every great guitarist from the era, but they were missing a gene factor from one particular great." I smiled. "It was controversial."

Machine-Head started to laugh and to gently sway from side to side.

"I'd say it was controversial," he chuckled.

"There was one guitarist from... What was that period, all those flowers and things?" I had to think hard.

"Zee sixties, dahling," cooed Lil. The eye opening in horror. "It could only have been then. I have seen all zee films, all those Beatles and Rolling things. And there was the one with my favoureet name. Same as his." She glanced up at the picture behind.

"Yeah," I said. "Of course. The sixties. Nineteen-sixties."

One of the Chickadees whistled. That was a long, long, *long* time ago.

"Astrodomus wanted this guitarist who had died long before the DNA Archive was set up by the Arts Council. So they programmed the feel, the emotion. . ."

I became aware of how meaningless this description probably was to the Chickadees; they wouldn't understand emotion in music. I only knew about it from my special studies. So I coughed and rethought.

"They took samples of this guy's old recordings and ran a simulation. It was controversial because it was physical DNA – real DNA. There are laws now. They made a Combo player, a real axeman made up from history's greats, and he headed one of the first Combo stomping bands."

"They called the dahling Jimi," hissed Lil. "I was so young then."

"The Combo got dismantled when the music industry switched completely to programmed music," said Machine-Head, with an arrogant sniff. "Someone smuggled the guitar out – we reckon this is it. I found it in an Off-Freeway antique joint in Upstate."

"How do you *'cut it'*?" asked the Chickadee with the beak-job. "What does that mean?"

I could sense that Machine-Head was getting hot. Flustered. Impatient with this example of today's youth which was taking up good space in Lil's office.

The keys around his head were steaming and, since they were direct into the nervo, I could tell that it was all getting too much for him.

"You little ignoramus. You play, that's what you do, you play it. You run your fingers up and down the frets and play. . ."

" 'Frets'?" asked a Chickadee.

" 'Play'?" said another.

Machine-Head thundered forward and pushed the kid out of the way. His huge hand swung down on to the neck of the guitar and, just as if it were a baby, he cradled it in his arms. OK, his fingers were fat, and he wasn't as nimble as he used to be, but even without amplo-feeding he was able to trip a riff off that fret board.

The Chickadee that Doc had been working on already had one of the UV implodes seeded; even though the synch wasn't tuned in he got a full blast directly into his system. The whites of his eyes sparkled.

For a few moments, time stood still as Machine-Head did his stuff. "Heyyy," he said, afterwards.

"It works," said Doc, looking smug.

Then a full flood of tears filled Machine-Head's eyes. "I used to play some," he said.

"Dahling," said Lil, tears welling up in her eyes, too.

The solo had been good. I even felt sad myself. I thought it was one by the man they called Eric Clapton.

She immediately went into power steer and pulled her wheels out from the Thatcher desk. With a flick of the auto-hover she cruised round to where the big hulk stood. She tugged at his rug jacket and he fell to his knees. The black-gloved hand pushed his head down on to her lap as he cried. She cradled his gleaming keys in her gloved hand. I'd never seen so many tears from a man so huge.

"You need a cuddle, that eez all. Come to me, my baby."

And I'll be darned if Soho Lil didn't actually kiss Machine-Head on the lips, right there and then.

I don't know if you've ever caught a shot of what it's like backstage during the Eurovision Song Contest? The Colosseum job in Rome was reputed to be the most crazy to date but I'm telling you the sub-contractors for the Trans-Med Stadium in West London didn't know what they were about.

There was talk that the MBI 0100's power supply was ropier than ever and most of the audience had brought their own modems, so the officials were yelling at everybody offering half-price deals. You couldn't hear yourself think the most basic tune.

The MBI 0100 computer, which hovered above everyone and ran the show, was huffing and puffing and couldn't stabilize. It hovered backwards and for-wards, threatening to fall on people's heads. As always, the cables caught up with some of the crowd and, on top of all that, an antiques fair was getting unloaded behind the disc-drive bank. When Lil's Chickadees came out of the testing station, there was nowhere for them to go; I mean, not even a climb-down parlour with Company Peace. So before they were wired up for stage presence, they hung around backstage with us.

It was running late. The French entry was a program called "A Leak in the Euro Tunnel". They were on before Lil's and one of the engineers was having problems with a computer virus.

Lil had parked with us backstage. There she was, in a new, bright, silver-plate hover with Machine-Head, who had brought along his new antique guitar to get it valued at the fair.

Machine-Head had been acting strange all week, talking to this guitar like it was human. Stroking the strings, reading through old early music history data on the CD Super Rom. He started on about *technique*. Technique! He kept singing, or trying to sing using words – you know, lyrics or something – and he was getting nostalgic and sloppy. He started to cry again and went on about how the business had been screwed up by industry and sponsorship and all that government stuff.

"Where is art?" he cried.

I mean – come on! Art, from the mouth of Machine-Head?

"Rock is business, dahling," said Soho Lil. "It was the natural successor to sport. All that aggro, it's got to go somewhere, baby."

Then Machine-Head asked Lil to sing the song that the guy in the picture above her desk was famous for –

she knows it, you see. She refused; well, it got so heavy, I had to leave, I just couldn't take it, but the Chickadees were real impressed and stayed all night asking questions about the guitarist Jimi Beckton.

Like I said, Machine-Head was still in this weird mode. He had this huge, floppy felt hat on and all these strings of java beads round his neck like he was some kind of old hippy. He looked crazy. He knelt beside Lil, who kept stroking the back of his neck with the tips of the glove.

Anyhow, the games. The Japanese team had been on earlier with a very good set which was played out to the MBI 0100 from a laptop. Some of the audience started to sway with the beat, the power lights of their modems swinging from side to side. Then the MBI 0100 refused further connection and disconnected.

I was supposed to be unbiased but I couldn't wait to see what Lil's Chickadees would do with Doc's new UV codes. Although we weren't "official audience", Lil managed to get a few extra mobile modems for us so that we could hook into the set, too.

Machine-Head was kneeling, quietly passing the chrome syringe from one hand to another. Frambo, the stage manager, and I fixed our hypodermics into the gland and plugged into our modems. I didn't want to miss this for anything. My neck felt sore, but after a moment or two, as I started to pick up, I got excited and the sting vanished.

The two Chickadees were being wired into their stage pods and the audience had become agitated and curious about there being live creatures beneath the MBI 0100 as a supplement to the programmed set. The Chickadees were being carefully positioned by an additional adjudicator whose job it was to ensure that the cabling was fair.

Out front it was beginning to sleet rain, but the crowd's enthusiasm still shone through the silver sheet. They remained firm, standing to attention with their modems. The kids gazed in wonder towards the stage, the UV glow burning from within the heave of composite, like a million LEDs. Melt-down fireflies danced along the spotlight paths and weaved in and out of the laser tractors, some of the audience at the front of the stage began a slow hand-clap; after all, they *were* being fussy on stage.

Then magic moments.

The lights out in the stadium dimmed. The laser pool which projected the seascape simulation across the stage engaged fire. A stream of swirling blue glow rolled into the paths of the Chickadees.

Soho Lil reached out and squeezed Machine-Head's arm; she was hot. But he still hadn't connected his modem as far as I could tell.

This was to be a big moment for Lil.

I clicked my control up a notch and squinted towards the light.

Frambo and I exchanged glances.

The UV implants which stood out from the bare, shiny heads of Lil's Chickadees glowed like hot coals within the heart of a fire.

Somewhere, Lil's program was run.

A synthesized percussive upbeat – a real neat run – hit me. A laser belt slapped across the heads of the audience.

There was an audible intake of breath from the seventy per centers out there.

I felt my ribs ache as if I'd received an unexpected kick from an old bass pedal.

I heard the audience moan, then cheer.

This was dyna-fission.

Then – they were off.

The Chickadees thought up a keyboard solo: it went straight up to the MBI 0100 and out into the modems.

Those implodes of Doc's worked! It felt as if my eyeballs had been pushed back into my head; my stomach turned over as if something powerful had exploded somewhere inside.

A keyboard run skidded up from the ends of my toes, meeting the percussion and a whole barricade of syntho-strings head on. I looked across at Frambo, but he was bent over, sneezing his head off with the sheer pleasure of it. Soho Lil was shaking in her chair, the hover-gyro shifting unsteadily from side to side.

The Chickadee with the beak-job twisted on his own bolts.

They had to win – they had to.

A star exploded inside my head.

Every nerve was stroked.

Above the crowd the MBI 0100 shuddered, the cables twisted, steam poured down from the vents.

It didn't like it. It didn't like it, *at all*.

Suddenly there was a dark sick hole as if someone had turned off the sun. I gagged from the shock – it was terrible, terrible. I felt cold – an icy wind cold as though I was being forced through a turkey climb-down. I could just about make out the shapes of the others around me, backstagers who appeared to be in a similar state of shock. Soho Lil's gloved hand reached out to Machine-Head, who, of course, couldn't tell what was happening; his modem remained unplugged.

Then I went into hallucinate.

It was bad. I went through it all – the worst kind of visions. Rotting meat opening up in my face. Maggots raining down on me.

Then, all that stuff, seeming to spurt through the MBI 0100's cables.

I heard myself scream. Then a sharp stabbing came, just behind the ear.

Norm mode flashed in. Frambo stood beside me with the hypo tube in his hand; he'd managed to disconnect me.

Frambo screamed at me.

"Overload! They've blown it, the MBI 0100's shut down mid-program. It hasn't even gone into Park. Lil'll go spare! They've crashed the computer!"

I slapped myself to bring myself back in.

"I went into hallucinate," I said, weakly.

"Of course," said Frambo. "A shut-down from an experience like that. Brilliant! But they didn't fuse the implodes. The whole of the Eurovision stadium is frozen in time; they're all in the middle of an experience which they can't finish!"

"Oh no," I moaned, thinking of Soho Lil's sterling.

I heard a growl. Machine-Head stood beside me. The metal of his voice sounded extra hard and angry. He stared up at the MBI 0100 and shook his fist.

"I curse the day that silicon chip and implode capsule screwed the mind of the world!"

His gaze searched for the antique fair lot.

"Is that an amplo-bank?"

"What?" asked Frambo.

"There, behind the disk-drive bank, is that an amplo-bank?"

Well, the cabinets had the word "Marshall" stamped across them and I knew something about all that old gear, so I nodded.

"Don't know if they work."

"May all the slugs of the world rain down on every synthesizer, disk-drive, modem, program, fax," (he paused and tried to remember some more), "Super CD Rom, calculator, cable, monitor. . . !" He screamed as he shook his fist again at the night sky.

The rain was falling heavier now and the felt hat was drooping on either side of his head. I'd never seen him like that. He reminded me of an ancient stomper called Dylan. Soho Lil had managed to disconnect and was staring in horror at the sobbing, wailing crowd.

"Let's do it," said Machine-Head, suddenly. "Let's get them out of this suspension with some real music."

Like a sniper mechanic, he picked up the black case

that he had brought with him, and with a single movement of one hand removed his hat. He reached into the case, picked up the bundle and slung the axe over his shoulder. Lil's mouth made a saggy circle, but no sound issued forth.

Frambo and I just watched; the guy had gone crazy.

He marched over to the Marshall stack and flicked some switches. The guitar had a radio sender customed in. He quickly snatched sight of the frequency from the games board and then strolled on to the stage like he owned the entire place.

Nobody tried to stop him – they were in awe.

The Marshall stack spat and fizzed for a moment, then the sound was automated into the implode frequency. He adjusted the radio signal to home in on the modems; if there was something in the electronics that would pick it up, then it would work. There usually was – some chip or other. It was a dirty line and the notes weren't perfect at first, but it didn't matter, because of what followed.

Machine-Head played.

I mean, he didn't send it from the grey-matter, or put in any cartridges, he actually *played* it into the Marshall and it bounced out into the audience. He used his fingers.

Drowned in emotion, Soho Lil tried to stand. She hadn't seen stage-stomping in years.

A trickle of notes, like delicate snowflakes danced out into the stadium.

Machine-Head came on strong and powerful with a strange, bright-yellow guitar that somehow dominated the entire stage. He played Jimi's axe.

Somebody mentioned something afterwards about seeing a giant figure of a man creep out from the shadows with a fleeting shape following.

Nobody could be quite sure what was happening.

Then, something primitive, raw and savage, sucked the very breath from the stadium itself.

Ancient memory, dormant in the wood of the instrument until now, became fired.

A single fork of light suddenly shot out across the crowd. It bounced back from every surface before curling in on itself, rounding and shaping, seemingly flying above their heads before diving down into the very heart of the spectators themselves.

They moaned with pleasure.

Above them, the laser-lens of the stage spotlights shattered into a snowstorm of glittering crystal which flowed out and down the path of golden light.

The bass thundered into a good strong foundation.

He was off! Sky-riding now!

Machine-Head did something I'd never seen before. He leapt into the air and landed in the splits, throwing the golden axe behind his head. A string of trembling tones squeezed out into the night. The crowd roared, floors shook, the stadium was transformed for moments into a powerhouse of solid sound.

They had unfrozen.

Soho Lil looked across at me; her face was wild.

The riff of thunder ripped across their heads, the Chickadees just watched – gob-smacked.

The yellow axe drove itself.

The MBI 0100 started up again, the cables thrashed, struggling to intercept the purity of Machine-Head's playing, running the disk hard now, but it was no competition.

Machine-Head's shadow grew upon the backdrop, stretching towards a level line with the MBI 0100. He became even more of a giant.

Then . . . it simply got weirder.

The propellor-like sweep of his arm appeared to engulf the curtains, the top part of his head appearing to increase in size like an inflating balloon, as if his hair was growing out into an enormous shock of tight curls.

The specially hired laser-gamma-lights, reserved for the finale, caught the machine heads of the axe.

Perfect shafts of light crossed the auditorium, catching the audience within its grip as the enormous rainbow net swept up the faithful. Salvation had arrived.

Almost immediately, there followed a screaming, grinding, jagged cut of a note. It whirled and twisted its way in and out and up and up, bathing the stadium with a thick pure tone.

Perfect tone.

Honest tone.

The same E-sharp that tuned the angels' harps, I guess.

The legendary lost harmonic, often softly spoken of by all great musicians – he had found it.

Machine-Head's fingers ran the length of the axe neck. They caressed, encouraged, loosened the easy flow of tumbling notes from the golden fretwork. A final chord hit the gently glowing pick-ups. It hung on the air, hovering for seconds, before thickening into a single bolt of white heat which shot out from the SG and pierced the heart of the MBI 0100.

The computer twisted into a fiery pyre.

Machine-Head's limbs became almost spider-like. He lifted the axe to his mouth. He seemed to darken – I mean, his skin actually became a dark veil. I thought for just a moment there was another guitarist up there.

"He's playing with his teeth!" yelled Frambo. "Only Hendrix ever did that!"

I heard Head cry out in response.

I saw it all from where I was standing.

The strings of the axe snapped out of the keys, and shot straight down his throat. They must have wrapped themselves around the pegs of his own keys because – he *became* the guitar!

The buttons of his shirt burst open and his chest gleamed a burning yellow, like the central glow of the pick-ups. The crowd gasped, they cried, they roared together.

The guitar solo of the century came out of his body.

We heard it. God's own rift.

He sang something. We caught a few words – about a colour, Lil said afterwards, about a Purple

Haze – just before he blew apart and the holy blood of the axe showered the front row of the Eurovision audience.

It was over. And Soho Lil chewed the two good fingers of her left hand off, she was so excited.

Machine-Head got deleted – decently cremated without any fuss. There wasn't even enough of him left to make a fifteen per center android. I got a special message amongst the usual E-mail fom Soho Lil. Being Madam Nostalgia herself and queen of the one liners, she'd sent me a cryptic note. It was a repro of the picture behind her desk; the inscription reminded me of the guy's name and she said that it was appropriate.

The pic was of one Jimmy Durante, a real old music-hall comedian. Of Machine-Head she only wrote:

"Eee found the lost chord, dahling. Geddit?"

It was certainly lost on me. But I got to keep the axe; Lill said I should have it. I worked out the rest for myself. The guy that owned that guitar was a composite of some really old greats. Who were they? Easy: Jimmy Page, Eric Clapton, Jeff Beck and, of course, Jimi Hendrix. Jimi Beckton indeed! I had to laugh. And I'm telling you something else. Those cigarette burns were for real. That wasn't no copy, that was some guitar – a real Gibson SG Special.

All Together

"It's like a mirror — but a mirror full of shadow-tinged rainbows," said Kaz, as she held the circular, silver disc at a tilt, just a little away from her.

The disc seemed almost magical, a drowning pool of images.

Reflected fluorescent light-fittings burned back from the edges of the circle. The rows of old vinyl records, neatly stacked on metal shelving, and the bright advertising posters filled the surface with a haze of colour.

Above this jazz of images, there seemed to float a patch of ever-changing pastels. Yellow and light blue bands which busily merged into one another. A further tilt of the disc and they would vanish, only to reappear on the opposing side. This time her own reflection peered back at her, just for a moment, before vanishing once again.

"Give it here," said Roger, as his arm reached over from the record counter. "Anyone would think that you'd never seen a compact disc before. These things are for playing, not staring into."

"But they sound so good, better than all your old vinyl," said Rib, who was busy poking his nose into the box which housed the latest CD releases for that month. "What I like most is not having to get out of my chair to turn the record over like in the old days, *and* I can program the tracks to play in whatever order I like."

Kaz sniffed as she reluctantly handed the CD back to Roger. She had only really wanted to check her make-up.

Then she caught sight of Rib's hand, seemingly frozen in front of his face, holding a plastic CD case inches from his nose. It seemed to mesmerize him.

"What have you got there?" she asked, wondering what had caught his interest.

"I don't know," he said, quietly. "It says it's a CD for 'up and coming young musicians'. That's the bit that interested me. That's us, isn't it? We're up and coming."

"Time will tell," sighed Roger, as he counted up the sales figures on his sheet, again.

"Let me look," said Kaz, snatching the plastic box from Rib's hand.

A crowd of faces stared back at her through the plastic.

"I like the cover. All those people, it's a bit like that Beatles album, 'Sergeant Pepper'. Not many sleeve notes, though. What's it say here?" She mused over the blurb. "Play-Along Disc. Play along-side the leading rock session musicians, learn new guitar licks, alternative rhythms, be tutored by those who *know*."

She looked up at Roger with a wrinkled, pained expression.

"What's a Play-Along disc?"

"You've found *that* in there, have you?" asked Roger, as his head reappeared from behind the shop counter. "I've got a poster to put out on that. It's a new idea – big promotion as well. Distributed by that huge London Megastore chain: you know, Pirate Records. They even offered me a dumpbin and leaflets, but that would be all too much for my little shop. It's difficult enough getting you lot to buy things. Thought I'd try a couple of copies, though, just to see how it went, specially since it's for *wannabe* musicians. Kind of karaoke, but you play instead of sing."

"We ain't *wannabes*," said Rib, seriously. "We're there already."

Roger raised an eyebrow.

"There's supposed to be other big promotions, too," he continued. "I guess it's a cross between a tutor and an excuse to put out some inedits – that's old cutting-room floor material to you. As I understand it from the distributor's release sheet, you accompany the tracks on the disc and learn new ideas. Nothing particularly unusual about that really, just a standard instrument tutor. Those things have been around for years. In fact, my kid brother learnt the piano from one. I've not listened to this yet; it's one of the first CD versions of a tutor I've heard of, they're usually cassette tapes or videos."

He thought for a moment.

"It's strange though, the way that something that ordinary is being pushed so hard. I don't even know who these 'top' session people are; it certainly doesn't tell you in the booklet. Wait a minute, I'll show you something."

He disappeared again behind his counter of junk.

After a moment he emerged with a large poster. One hand searched for Blu-tack as the other tried to spread the sheet out on the wall beside the counter.

"Been meaning to put this up. It's just a replica of the sleeve, but I think it looks quite good."

Rib stared at the poster. It showed a crowd of waving people looking upwards towards the viewer. They were mostly youngsters, all shapes and sizes and ages, all in different kinds of dress. Just a regular group. They were smiling. Some held guitars, others waved drumsticks or held keyboards neatly tucked under their arms like daily newspapers. He didn't recognize anybody, not even any famous musicians, although the sleeve notes of the CD did say "Play alongside the leading rock session musicians".

Kaz thought that the picture might have been taken at an airfield. On a concrete runway, perhaps. There were small, painted white blocks on either side of the assembled crowd, like road markings, and there was nothing else for what seemed like miles around. In an arc above the head of the group was the title: PLAY ALONG. ALL TOGETHER. In the corner of the poster a large black hat sat above a dark eye patch and a rough, partly grown beard. The other eye was open –

a gleaming watching orb. Beneath this were the words: *Pirate Records Ltd. A splendid time is guaranteed for all. Come and listen to the best band in the world.* And below this in capital letters: ARE YOU GOOD ENOUGH TO PLAY WITH US?

Kaz wasn't quite convinced.

It all seemed just too cosy. They seemed to be smiling *too* much. She also wasn't sure that the splendid time promised would be that splendid.

Rib felt different. Something told him that he should buy it and give it a try. It seemed a peculiarly attractive proposition for reasons he couldn't understand. Perhaps it was vanity? The challenge? What exactly did it mean by "Are you good enough. . ."?

Of course he was good enough and he would rise to any challenge!

He stared at the poster again, searching the faces in the crowd. There was something about them.

Were they beckoning rather than waving?

He wondered.

Suddenly, a loud "clang" disturbed his thoughts. He almost leapt out of his skin.

The old shop-bell had suddenly jangled its announcement of the entry of new customers. They hated the bell, left over from the time that Roger's shop had been a grocery store, but Roger refused to take it down. After all, it was old and original. Just like Roger.

A black leather-jacketed figure, with long arms and legs waving like a huge, dark insect's mandibles, stalked into the shop.

It was Terry, the bass player, followed by "Spider" Josh.

As usual, Terry's personal stereo was glued to his ears, holding his black, gelled, spiky hair in place like a metallic hair net. Close behind, appearing to shadow-box his way in through the doorway (but without a personal stereo) strutted Josh. He wore the familiar dark glasses, with a thin trail of dreadlock plaits tumbling out from beneath a huge, knitted beret.

Josh didn't need any headphone music, he was the best drummer on the estate.

All of the band met in Roger's shop at Saturday lunchtimes. Roger would suggest new titles for them to listen to, help the guys increase their repertoire, sometimes even lend them records for the weekend. Roger was a good mate.

Roger was about to call out his usual "Hi there, Spider man," greeting, but instinct stopped him from doing so.

Things were not quite right.

It was the sudden mask that had dropped quite unexpectedly beneath his personal stereo. It had happened as soon as he had entered the shop. This was not their usual entrance; even Josh stopped shadow-boxing to the music as he closed the door behind them, but he had also seen what had caught Terry's eye.

"Heh, Josh," whispered Terry. "Come here and cop this; there's even one in Roger's shop."

The OFF button on the little plastic box strapped to

his belt was clicked with a quick firm movement. The tinny beat stopped.

Terry's eyes stared out ahead of him, past his friends. They betrayed a strange fascination.

He was staring at the newly displayed poster.

For a moment he said nothing. He merely walked directly up to the bizarre, waving assembly and looked long and hard at the figures. A single finger traced the faces in the crowd. Slowly, he began to shake his head from side to side.

"It's that Play-Along CD." He raised his voice and called over his shoulder. "We've seen this before, haven't we, Josh? Up town, at the Pirate Megastore in Oxford Street. They were everywhere, or so it seemed. So you're stocking it here, eh?"

Terry's eyes remained on the poster, continuing their scan of the waving figures.

Roger wondered what was wrong.

"Have any of you heard it yet?" he continued.

"What's the matter, Tel?" asked Kaz, taking a particular sudden interest.

She stopped flicking through the records.

Terry ignored her question.

"Remember those ones we saw in Pirate's, Josh?"

Josh sloped over, removed his dark glasses to a point just an inch above his nose and scrutinized the sheet.

"Relax man, you're making too much of this. At least they ain't fighting."

Roger had stopped working on his figures and was

now watching all of this with an interest which grew by the second.

"Fighting, fighting with who? Would one of you tell me just what's going on? What's this all about?"

Josh lowered his glasses back on to the bridge of his nose.

"Tel and me we went into Pirate's last week," he began. "You know, just to look around. This CD was in there, it was everywhere." He grinned. "Causing a real sensation; the centre of attention, you might say."

"There was trouble," said Terry. "Funny trouble. In fact, a bundle was going on at the enquiries desk."

"Three boys, right," interrupted Josh, "were being given a real hard time by the security guards. We think the kids were in a group and some of them had bought copies. We didn't take a lot of notice at first, but then it got rough. It ended with one kid getting frogmarched off by three guards."

"Happens all the time," shrugged Roger.

"No, this was really serious. I mean, it seemed like he'd committed a bad crime. What bugged us was that they were saying strange things. One kid was yelling about how they'd nearly lost their friend because of the thing, and what did Pirate Records think they were playing at and so on."

"What was it one of them said?" asked Josh, trying to remember. "That odd comment, 'couldn't have him' or something? Yeah, that was it: 'they couldn't have him'. Man, was he making a fuss!"

" 'Couldn't have him'?" repeated Kaz.

"Is that it? Is that all?" asked Roger.

Terry and Josh looked at one another, then Josh continued.

"You weren't there. Those security guards went over the top with these kids. One of them, a really heavy guy with this peaked cap, told them to keep their mouths shut if they knew what was good for them! So I said to Terry, 'There's more to this than meets the old eye.' Terry grabbed one of the kids outside before he ran off, asked him what was wrong. He was almost in tears, didn't want to talk at first but then he said something really strange."

Josh shifted uneasily from one foot to another. He swallowed hard.

"He looked straight at us. The kid was in another world. Said that he couldn't play the guitar any more, his mate couldn't even tap out a simple snare drum and it was all the fault of this Play-Along disc. Then he said that they couldn't make them join if they didn't want to, could they? It was a sort of frightened question. He ran off before we could get any more."

Josh looked directly at Terry.

"But it was his eyes," he whispered, "his damn eyes. Open, empty, frightened. He was scared. *Real* scared."

There was a dark, icy silence that almost dripped fear. Despite the bright sunshine of the day, the shadowy corners of the shop seemed to reach out towards them. The fun had gone out of the Saturday lunchtime meet.

Kaz shivered.

"Stop it, you lot, you're giving me the creeps."

Rib grinned. "You almost had me going then."

Terry and Josh remained stone-faced.

Roger leant over to the box of new releases. After a few flicks through the plastic squares he found a copy of the Play-Along CD.

"Those West End security guards have a difficult job sometimes, you know. I'm sure there was an explanation. Anyhow, let's give it a spin, as we used to say."

After checking the serial number, Roger reached back amongst his shelves and removed a cardboard sleeve. A sparkling silver disc flopped out into his hand.

He punched a button beneath the counter, and they heard the whirring of a smoothly geared CD tray offering its tongue to receive the silver disc.

For a moment there was a velvety silence. No hiss, no crackle. No pop. Just pure digitized silence.

After a few seconds, a rough growl of a DJ hype voice thudded across the tiny shop.

"Hi, there! The Pirate Records Corporation welcomes you to the best band in the world. Enjoy good sounds while learning the newest, sweetest, *hottest* licks around, all on your own chosen instrument. You'll be taught by the men in the shadows. We want you to be relaxed and serious about your special tuition. This is a precision disc, computed to help you learn and *play along*. For this purpose you need to be alone when you play and listen. We want your attention. We *need* your attention. Exclusively. OK? One moment now while we run a check."

Roger's eyebrows knitted into a serious frown.

"Run a check? What do they mean run a check?"

The group looked at one another.

The disc tinkled within the player.

After a few moments the voice returned.

"Sorry, folks! We have computed that there are more than the permitted amount of listeners in the room. I'm afraid the tuition part of this disc cannot proceed at present. In the meantime please enjoy a selection of top cuts played exclusively for you by the Play-Along band."

A synthesized rhythm bounced into the shop.

Roger stared down at the player.

"That's the tune we heard in Pirate's, it was played in the store," said Josh. "Only this one sounds different..."

"Louder?" asked Rib.

"Quiet, man," said Josh. "Let me listen. It's a fuller sound, perhaps there are more musicians ... I don't know."

Roger ejected the disc. His brow was stuck in a single expression. He couldn't believe it, it had to be a joke. All these years in the business and he orders an album that was choosy about when it wanted to be played?

He threw the silver disc on the counter. They should have stuck with vinyl. There was an awkward silence for a few minutes. Rib had gone strangely quiet.

"I want to buy a copy," he said, suddenly. "I want to hear it at home."

His eyes were glazed.

"Rib?" asked Kaz.

"*I'm* good enough, after all," he continued.

Roger was startled for a moment but quickly picked up the disc and placed it beneath the counter.

"Oh, no. I'm not having you waste your money. In any case, there's something about this I need to check out. This is going back where it came from." Roger's eyes shifted from side to side; his sixth sense had kicked in.

Rib stared up at the poster in silent fascination and wonder. He wanted to Play-Along, badly. So badly, but he couldn't understand why.

A crescent smile of white teeth gleamed at him beneath the dark sightless patches of drop-hood shades. The huge security guard's folded arms reinforced the impression of someone who might just be the Keeper of the Secret Gate, but this uniform was only responsible for the Oxford Street branch of Pirate Records, and only the Rock section at that.

Rib had felt strangely nervous about entering the store. There was, of course, the inner guilt about not buying the CD from Roger's shop. He needed the business badly, but what could he do? Roger, for some reason, wouldn't sell him a copy and had already returned the two that he had previously ordered as shop stock.

Finding the Play-Along disc had been more difficult than he had imagined. Terry and Josh had said that they were all over the store. Dozens of them packed loosely into dumpbins.

Now there was no sign of them.

"That was a special offer last week," said a blue-lipsticked, pale-faced store assistant. "The dumpbins have been withdrawn. I don't even know whether we've got any copies left at all."

"But why? I thought it had only just been released. There were loads of them here last week."

"Well, that was then and this is now. They've all gone. We've been told to withdraw the rest of the stock. I only work here part-time; I sing in a band, you know."

The assistant continued to put out the records.

"But you must have one copy somewhere?" persisted Rib, who now seemed agitated.

The security guard in the corner of the CD section turned his fixed, crescent smile in Rib's direction. He had heard the anguished conversation and he had a nose for trouble.

The arms unfolded.

"Like I said, I only work here," said the assistant. "We're out of stock and the reorder sheets just kept coming back marked something like *enough taken*."

"*Enough taken?*" repeated Rib. "What's that mean?"

"Search me. Like I said, I only work here."

The girl shrugged her shoulders and was about to return to her task of putting out new releases in the racks when she was brought face to face with the security guard. He had swiftly and silently glided over.

"Everything all right?" asked the guard.

Rib felt a shiver bristle the hairs on the nape of his neck.

"The ... the Play-Along CD. You had it here last week, on display. I ... I wanted a copy, that was all."

For a moment the grin disappeared. The guard looked Rib up and down. The dark drop-shades lifted for a second as the face nodded at something or someone across the shop floor. Rib turned round to see who he could have been nodding at, but then, quite suddenly, a huge laugh tumbled out from a place within the blue uniform.

"OK Penny, I'll handle this," he said to the assistant.

An over-heavy hand slapped Rib on the back, as the guard's face lowered to his. Then he whispered in Rib's ear.

"Are you sure now? Are you *good enough*, if you know what I mean?"

Rib found himself smiling in return. He felt bathed in a warm comforting waft of air. Perhaps it was the shop's air-conditioning.

"Sure," he replied. "I'm good enough."

"Wait here, son," said the guard. "You seem like

a nice kid, eh? Perhaps I can find just one more copy."

The room had been darkened.

Just ever so slightly.

The light which Rib usually shone down on to his turntable was now turned upwards, casting a widening ray of light across the wall. A moth fluttered and teased the opening of the shade, throwing gentle shadows within its wake.

Rib inhaled deeply whilst cracking his knuckles. He sat before the keyboard of his Yamaha X5000 synthesizer. Waiting and wondering.

It was almost like a dare, a dare with himself. With his parents out at the pub and the rehearsal for that night cancelled, the moment was just right. Opportune. Perhaps he should have told Roger that he'd got the last copy of the Play-Along CD from Pirate's, but he had been so strict about wanting to return the things to the distributors. He'd said that records or CDs should play when *you* wanted them to, not when *they* felt the moment was right.

But Rib had to try it out for himself.

The conditions outlined in the booklet had been met: he was relaxed and on his own.

His left hand reached for the infra-red remote control for his Wakaki 7000; a single squeeze aimed in the direction of the CD player started the disc. A gentle tinkle, like a far off wind-chime, announced that the disc was being read.

The light seemed to darken, almost as if there had suddenly been a mains dip. The CD player's digitized LED lights glowed. A deep voice cut through the gloom, not quite entering the room from the accurately set stereo speakers. It was more as if the voice had arrived from beneath the floor-boards.

But then suddenly, like a bolt from the blue, it was everywhere, below him and all around the room.

"Hi, there. Well, that's better, that shop was stuffy!"

Rib blinked.

"Let's see what you can do then. A simple 12-bar boogie coming up; just get into the beat and let your fingers trickle out those notes. Just . . . Play-Along, all together!"

The crisp snap of a Hi-Hat cracked out of the darkness. A full-throated sound filled the room, led by a guitar intro that just begged for a bass run from the lower octave of the Yamaha.

The rhythm was infectious.

Rib was swept up with the beat. His fingers simply raced across the keys, filling in with complex runs and trills that he had never even dreamt he could handle. He was removed from time and space. The fourth dimension of sound had just seemed to open out there and then in the living-room, enveloping his body and mind.

A voice from the CD said, "Yeah!"

Rib replied, "You've got it!"

The shadow of the moth fluttered its crazy whirl of shapes across the wall, the dark patches appearing to bounce and flicker with the beat. Even the CD player, which usually glowed quite innoculously within the music centre, seemed to throb and tremble with the rhythm.

The voice-over suddenly cut in.

"Hey, that's real neat! You sure can cut it! OK, let's give it some beef, eh? See what you can *really* do."

He took the lead.

Rib turned up the volume on the Yamaha. Even though he was playing through a practice amplifier, the throaty bass shook the empty mugs which sat out on the kitchen drainer.

His hands lifted into the air for a few moments, large hovering spiders, and then lunged suddenly into the river of synthetic ebony and ivory. The keys caressed his fingertips.

"Hey!" came the voice-over. "You're excellent! Do you want to join the band, the best band in the world, do you?"

Rib continued playing. It was a crazy method but the encouragement and the music was fantastic.

The voice returned. "I SAID – DO YOU WANT TO JOIN THE BEST BAND IN THE WORLD? LET ME HEAR YOU! YOU'VE GOTTA MEAN IT!"

Rib laughed. It was as if it was talking to him personally.

The trickle of sweat down his back chilled.

"LET ME HEAR YOU, BOY! LET ME HEAR YOU! ARE YOU GOING TO PLAY ALONG OR JOIN? WE

WANT YOU! ARE YOU GOOD ENOUGH? LET ME HEAR YOU SAY IT! GIVE ME YOUR SOUL, BROTHER!"

"Yeah!" cried Rib. "I'm good enough!"

"Fantastic!" came the reply. "OK, let's go. ALL TOGETHER NOW, alltogethernow!"

The CD motor engaged overdrive, turbo drive, ultimate drive.

The voice-over increased in volume, and as it did the same repetitious phrase was repeated, over and over and over again.

"Alltogethernow, alltogethernow, alltogethernow!"

Faster and faster. Faster and faster.

"Alltogethernow, alltogethernow!"

The rainbow secrets of the silver disc spilled out from the disc drawer. They rushed and swept a pathway of golden light around the room, darting between the notes which fluttered and bounced around the four walls.

The CD drawer smoothly opened like the well-greased drawbridge of a magic castle. The occupants floated out.

At first it appeared to Rib as if the CD player had become transformed. As the drawer opened, small shining orbs of multicoloured light appeared to float up and away from the tray, just like soap bubbles. There were only a few small bubbles at first, but then, as the tempo of the music increased, so did the size of the orbs. It was as if the disc had expanded and inflated from its usual flat, silver platter.

A rolling flow of swimming melting colour just passed in front of his keyboard.

Rib stared into it.

There was movement.

Someone or something was inside. It jerked, shuddered like an infant or a creature in an egg.

His jaw slackened; he stopped playing.

Behind the ever-changing rainbow screen, a figure twisted and turned. A kid about his own age, furiously thrashing for all he was worth at a drum set. Other orbs followed, all containing young musicians with saxophones, keyboards or other instruments, but they were somehow different. It was something about the slit of their eyes and the length of their nails.

Rib pushed the keyboard away from him. His eyes anxiously searched for the door. He hadn't noticed the empty bubble which had been slowly drifting around to the back of the room. The soft, yielding, soapy film wrapped itself around him; something pulled him into its embrace.

He was taken away in a shimmering orb of colour and sound, playing with the best band in the world, the men in the shadows.

He *was* good enough.

When Rib awoke, he found himself lying at a very awkward angle just in front of the settee. Kaz shook him hard; he had been raving. She had intended to make a social call and as the front door was on the latch she had let herself in.

"What is it, what's the matter?" She shook him hard again.

Rib didn't answer at first. His eyes were wild and searching.

He felt cold and empty inside.

The living-room light had now been switched on. The spaghetti tangle of cables and leads from his Yamaha had knotted around his feet.

He tried to get up, but fell back against the settee again.

"A dream ... dream? They can't make me join ... can they?" he mumbled.

"Wait a minute," said Kaz. "I'm going to get you a drink. I don't know what's been going on here. Look at the place."

She swiftly disappeared through the door and out into the kitchen. Rib peered across at his CD deck with half-closed eyes. The drawer was open. Staggering on to his feet he stretched out his hand towards the player and lifted the silver disc out of the drawer.

It had a wet, sort of *soapy* feeling.

Then he noticed a single small bubble on the fire-side rug, shimmering for a few seconds before finally bursting into a mucous-like slime, like the trail of a snail.

Rib left the band almost immediately.

The rest of them agreed that the very life had gone out of his playing. Almost as if his drive had been suddenly drained. Terry reckoned that he just couldn't play any more, that he had simply lost interest and that was that. He just didn't want to play.

Kaz had thought that it might have something to do with finding him in such a state that night.

Now they had all been summoned to Roger's shop, just after closing time. Roger had said that it was important and that Rib shouldn't know about it. They all stood before Roger's counter, wondering what this could all be about. Perhaps he'd found a replacement for Rib, or a recording contract at long last.

Roger looked grave. He had just locked the front door and twitched the venetian blind closed.

To the right of the counter was the Play-Along CD poster, one corner flapping over from insufficient Blu-tack. He had put it back up for some reason.

Roger coughed. He looked bothered, almost nervous.

"This is rather stupid. But it bothered me and I wanted to find out what you lot thought. Just for you to tell me that it's my stupid imagination." He pointed at the CD poster.

"Well?" asked Kaz. "What about it?"

Roger reached behind the counter and brought out a small, brown paper bag. Carefully he opened one end and retrieved a small plastic case. It was a compact disc.

"I sent my copies of this Play-Along thing back," he said, "but last week, unsolicited, five new copies arrived. There was a press release sheet with them. *The Play-Along band is bigger and better than ever.*

112

New over-dubbing with added musicians. That's what it said. The music certainly has a fuller sound now. But. . ."

He paused.

"Take a look at the cover for me."

Roger passed the plastic case over to Kaz. Terry and Josh huddled at her right shoulder.

At first they couldn't see what was wrong, but Spider Josh snapped his glasses right off and kept glancing at the poster and then the CD cover. Then back to the poster again.

"What is it?" asked Terry. "I don't see anything wrong."

"Look, man," cried Josh, "on the new cover. The crowd's bigger, more people. There's hundreds of them!"

"So?" asked Terry.

But then he caught sight of Kaz's wide-eyed expression.

"No!" she gasped. "Surely not?"

Her finger carefully traced the faces on the cover but then stopped at a new figure who was waving from the very front of the crowd. She glanced back at the wall but the face wasn't there on the poster. She peered back at the CD cover. She squinted her eyes up tight.

The new figure was waving and smiling.

Kaz hurriedly snapped open the CD case and stared at the flat, silver disc. Just as she tilted it, it caught the light: the fluorescent lights, the shelving with stacks of records and then a boy's head flashed briefly from within the rainbow stripe.

It had been a familiar face gazing from behind a Yamaha keyboard.

They were all together now. And this time it was easier to notice the white chalked pentacle that they were all standing within.

Liquid Friendship

"I wanted some.

"I wanted some and I wanted it *now*. And I usually get what I want, don't I?

"You know how it is. Sometimes you've just gotta have it.

"I've tried most things: corkers, pacifiers, buzz-flies, magik moments, as well as samples of stuff they dish out at the Social Mediation Centres that give you 'rainbow' spots. But that's just tame gear, isn't it? We all know that; I mean, it's not the real thing. And you have to listen to all this social-worker chatter about how they'll help you review your place in society.

"Give me a break! They think that legalizing Raves and organizing it all for you is gonna make some kind of difference. It's like going to a birthday party your mum organized for you. Pha! We still want the secret places, we don't want no State-organized bull.

"You see, I'm the kind of kid that needs the real banana.

"You have to understand something here. I'd heard. I knew. It was out there, you just had to do what you had to do to go get it. But I didn't know how to access it, OK?

"Then I happened on the route, just by accident.

"There was this kid, right. He stopped me in the Mall. I was cruising – thinking of a late night shopping bash if Kaz had managed to jump an auto and was prepared to do the business. I knew this kid from some blag he'd fenced for us and he told me he'd been getting some info. He surfed the Net, this kid; man, he was a real cyberhead and I wondered if perhaps the word was coming in from there.

"But, no. It wasn't.

"Then he spilled.

"He'd had word from the Blackwater Flats crowd. He reckoned they knew about it, too, you know – accessing the real banana.

"Hey – those guys! Eh? Those guys!

"They've made some news lately, gotta give it to them, the Blackwater Flats kids are the biz. Everyone knows they get you blue-boys on the hop, even get you out in your noddy shields and shiny heads with those flashy new batons and real cool little shades you wear that make your boys look like Jean-Paul Gaultier on a good day. That was a laugh – chased your lot clear through the estate and round the precinct shopping veranda, on a Saturday morning, too!

" 'Go make a word and say I sent you,' says this kid.

" 'I don't need to say you sent anything to anyone,' I said, with this real good look in my eye. I turned up the collar on my Gucci shirt and flashed my fake Rolex in his face.

"I had my own way in, see.

"There's this femmy, and she was in with them. The Blackwater Flats kids. She'd tell them I was cool and if my informer was on the ball they'd tell what the word is on this stuff. So I thought I'd make my way to the top car park of the Merchant Street Mall and find out what's going down.

"Lemme just tell you about her, for a minute, OK?

"She calls herself Tick-Tock and apart from having a real cute name, she's a dream canoe. She's got this white stripe in her hair – like a badger – black vampire eyes and a real cool ring in her nose. But it was the other touches that did it for me.

"I oggled her fairly recently when I saw her sitting on the wall outside the perimeter fence that they've ringed round the Flats. It was true love at first sight. She was cooler than a penguin's freezer, with this real neat hat with blue pipe lining and this green elastic gusset at the back. She wore knee-length socks with designer Fabricci tops. Then there were these roller blades. They looked brand new, and she was just fixing a second one on to her foot. They were great. Red leather, clearly label stuff – Fernando's, I thought, though they might have been some cheap Paul Morley stock. I dunno. Anyhow, the laces were white nylon, cross-string design with a sewn-in black line side that I'd not seen before. Anyway, doesn't matter about the gear, if you're interested I'll tell you later. She was real, real, *real*.

"I was full of confident feelings, you know; I felt sure of the certainty of certainty, so I gave it my best shot.

"I said, 'Where'd you get them, then, done some shopping recently?'

"She knew I had the oggle for her, even though she blew me out with a dreamy look that simply said 'Go bore somebody else.'

" 'Bet you've got some cards?' I say to her.

"She shakes her head.

"I put my hand in my back pocket and produce about half a dozen, then I fan them like I'm David Hart – that hot but seedy American magician on TV. They spread like a peacock's tail, but prettier.

"This little trick gets femmies real hot, honest; any chance to blow some stolen plastic with you and they drool down your neck. Her eyes go wider than the headlights on a vintage Porsche.

"I follow this up with some great conversation, a real cool piece about her roller blades, and how the real perfecto laces made them something exclusively distinctive in a socially vacant world, immune to the niceties of good design.

"She said I was full of el crapo, and we laughed. But it did the biz.

"We went out places for a bit, and I knew she was in with this gang of pleasure-seekers, so it couldn't last, you had to live on the Flats to belong. We did the usual great stuff, we hung out at burger bars and managed to collect all the little plastic keyring Burger Men from the MacHughes' chain, the ones you get with the extra chocolate extra Super Shakes and the free burger with extra fries. I could never belong to the Blackwater

Flats kids though, that's what she said. Territory was territory.

"So, I blew my mind when this kid tells me that the word on the streets is that the Blackwater guys know the way, the truth and the light.

" 'Amen to that!' That's what I said.

"So I thought, OK let's face to face with Tick-Tock and her little friends and see if I can nuzzle my way in.

"I found them right where the kid told me I would. Man, they had some great gear. San Francisco Peter Small T-shirts, with Sandre Greco balloon-style pants, and half of them had these Gucci shades with the silver-lined arms at the sides. They looked truly wary when they saw me crossing the roof-top. There weren't many cars about, legit shoppers are getting wise to the problem of leaving your wheels on the top drawer. One guy was skating up to the edge where that car went over; they hadn't bothered to repair the wall and he was dicing with it! So cool. Tick-Tock saw me and smiled, but I knew she was antsy about my being there. She assured the others I was OK with a sultry look and slinked over.

" 'What's happening?' I said. I hadn't seen her for a while, see.

"Tick-Tock shook her head and wagged her finger at me, like she was a parent or something.

" 'You shouldn't be here – this is family, you know that.'

"So I go for it.

" 'Word's out that the Blackwater Flats guys know

what's going down, that there's to be this Rave, a special to introduce their new product.'

"I grinned. I cracked my face from ear to ear.

"She went very quiet for a moment and toyed with the ring in her nose. She looked great. Behind her I could see the Blackwater Flats kids giving me the big eye. Ordinarily I'd have been out of there, they were pacing like you know they're going to strike. But I was with Tick-Tock so I knew that it'd be dandy.

"'What do you know about our new product?' she said.

"'Only that it's something big. The ultimate in iced heaven. Word's out that there's never been anything like it. Supposed to make Raves something really special.'

"She stuck out her tongue and licked the top of her lip. That meant she was thinking. I'd got to know Tick-Tock well, so I'd learned her unique style of body language.

"'It's colder than iced heaven,' she said, casual like.

"I whistled.

"'That cool?'

"'It's a stack of freezers.'

"I just said, 'I want part of the action.'

"She turned on her heels and snaked back over to the rest of the guys. She spoke for a while to one of them. This was some big dude with a Moss Bros top hat he'd customized with a Carlos Portillo headscarf. It was an excellent idea.

"Then the two of them came over.

" 'Tick-Tock says you're OK,' he began. 'You have an interest in our new product.'

"I nod, saying nothing, though.

" 'So what do you know about it?'

" 'That it's the big banana.'

"He cut in with a whiny voice I wasn't expecting.

" 'Don't fruit-talk me, man. This is bigger than that. It's a group experience.'

"For a moment I wasn't sure what he was putting down here. I mean, everything we take at Raves and things are group experiences, aren't they? We dance and dance till our bones rattle and our brains are jellies in a two-windowed apartment. We just trip the rainbow with fried eggs heaping up on our skulls. It's a social event after all, isn't it?

" 'How do you mean, it's a group experience?' I was feeling braver; this sounded like the usual stuff.

"The man went dark.

"I mean, his whole apperance goes gothic, and he somehow seems larger than life itself as we know it.

" 'Every new product needs testing. We'll contact you about the test site. Enough for you to know it was brought in last month from Europe, came through the tunnel.'

" 'Let me have something,' I said. 'Just a word?'

" 'It's a patch, with a capsule inside. You stick it on the back of your neck, hold this patch in place and then there's a small wire that you pull. It releases the goodies, goes through the skin, straight into the body through the nervous system.'

"So I gasped. I'd never heard of this before.

" 'And it socializes?' I asked. 'You mean, you dance better?'

"I wasn't getting any handle on this thing, other than how good it was. Tick-Tock and this guy laugh. Tick-Tock flashes this look at me, her eyes grew big, the irises almost throbbed.

" 'Yeah, you dance better. You do everything better.'

"Then this dude takes off his top hat and runs his fingers through this close-cropped hairstyle. He brushes the velvet coat of his hat and adjusts the scarf, and sniffs.

" 'Liquid friendship,' he said, quietly, like it was some dark secret.

"I blink. I mean, a real deep blink. I'd heard of this stuff; there was some talk going round on the Net and elsewhere too, but it was all legend, never supposed to have existed in the real world.

" '*Liquid friendship*,' I repeated; they knew I'd heard of it. 'I mean,' I went on, 'are we talking the stuff that melts all barriers, makes you the centre of the earth, the core?'

"They both nod. I pushed my fist into the air. They had this gear and my femmy was in on it.

" 'Get it straight,' says the dude with the hat. 'It's action is more specific, it's a friendly product. We go one step at a time. Tick-Tock's spoken well of you. You can see – but for now you don't get to touch. No deals yet.'

122

"I didn't see much of Tick-Tock after that. I knew that it was security. I carried my mobile everywhere and went to ground myself, in case the connection with Tick-Tock went down on the street and I'd be sniffed at for a preview of the deal. I wasn't too much of a surfer – either real time or Compu-mail – but I stopped at the occasional cybercafé to access and see what was going down. There was cable chatter everywhere. They were running teaser ads – you know the kind: *'Liquid Friendship – the bond that is stronger'*, *'Become one with the spirit'*, *'You're not alone – Friendship is here'*, and a gaggle of others.

"Then I get this call, right?

"It came late, and I wasn't expecting the thing at all; I thought I was going to get some E-mail message or something, or maybe just a note passed to me on the street. But no, I get this call straight into my mobile. It's just a number. I call it, and I get an answerphone message to call this other number and order pizza. I call it, I order the pizza – Iced Heaven. They give me an order number. So it goes.

"Then after an hour I hit bingo.

"The product launch was to be at this warehouse, right. I was told to be ready at the bridge and they'd take me downriver in the back of this truck. Man, there were loads of them. Every one who was anyone on the street was there, all standing like cattle in the back of these farm truck things. Hellzapoppin knows where they got them from, but that's the Blackwater Flats guys for you.

"I got picked up in the second truck. It was an old part of Docklands before the Crash of the century cleared it out. The atmosphere was a stunner and I was jam-packed with all these other heads.

"You could hear the sounds as we crossed the river. It was a big warehouse with neat Conran designed windows. A blue blade of light cut through these venetian shutters like lasers. You just knew that it was all happening in there like they promised. It was like glimpsing inside Pandora's Box.

"At the door I was given this patch, like a small plaster, and a bottle of sparkling Perrier water, fortified with a glucose designer sugar tab. Man, we raved like the kingdom was dawning. Tick-Tock was there already. She crossed the floor, the light picking up on her stripe making her seem like a jag of lightning.

"But she seemed all wrong.

"You've asked me to describe this to you before and I can't. It was like a heat haze. It was damn hot in there, but it was more a visual thing, like watching a room of chocolate ice-cream melt. I'd fixed my patch but hadn't pulled the thread that released the gear. I was saving myself – I wanted to go through to the next morning.

"The light was brighter than a neutron bomb. And Tick-Tock kind of stepped out of it. She held me close and then I felt her fingers on the back of my neck. There was a slight pricking sensation, and then I thought I might be bleeding, my neck felt wet. She'd pulled the wire.

"And then she kissed me.

"Her lips were honey; man, I thought I was tasting a dessert served to a god. Somebody held my hand, then another, then. . .

"I . . . I find this difficult.

"It was then that I realized the thing about Tick-Tock's fingers, the thing that I couldn't understand. Well, they were stroking the back of my neck. It was real cool, it was fun.

"She was standing real close to me. For a moment it was as though we might be naked. I kind of liked it and didn't pay it no attention.

"Then I felt her again, up near my neck.

"But it was when I thought I felt her fingers *inside* my jaw that I balked. How was that possible? They crept round and then she was feeling the inside of my lips with her nails; I felt her palm inside my cheek and then those fingers again – reaching out to caress my brain through the roof of my mouth!

"I glanced to my left. Some guy seemed to be dancing on three legs. Then he kind of dissolved.

"Oh, God – where did they get that stuff?"

The policeman leaned forward and spoke into the tape recorder microphone.

"Interview terminated, 12.15 hours. Suspect distressed."

The Incident-Scene squad had approached the warehouse with extreme caution. The kid had been

125

interviewed all night about the event and the same story kept coming through: some new street-socializing drug that made some kind of bond between dancers at illegal Raves.

Chief Inspector Collins had seen many things in his long and distinguished career, and had put together the best team he had available. But nothing prepared him for the state of his fellow officers as the car pulled up at the wharf-side.

A paramedic's team had been there for hours already, but the casualties had been the investigating officers.

Collins had brought the kid with him. He leapt out of the police car and two other officers helped the kid out of the back. The kid kept complaining of feeling sick, and being uncomfortable across his shoulders.

"Where the hell are they all, where have they gone?" Collins called.

A squad detective with a face paler than a bed sheet approached Inspector Collins.

"Be warned when you go in there, sir. Be very careful and prepared."

"I thought someone was pulling a fast one," said Collins. "I mean, I was getting ridiculous information through on the radio."

In the distance, another policeman staggered out of the warehouse door. He looked as though he was about to be sick, and leaned against a nearby wall.

Collins marched up to the entrance with a determined pace. He nodded at the officer who was supporting himself against the wall.

Collins opened the door and went in.

There was little natural light inside. The blinds were drawn on most of the windows. But halogen lamps had been rigged at the sides of the huge empty space. Disco equipment stood unused and alone at the end of the room. Huge speakers were rigged on to the cross beams. Then, in the gloom of the shadows, he saw what at first he thought was an enormous mattress. It lay in humps, spread out upon the floor and filled most of the space. But near where he stood it fragmented into sections, seeming to bubble and heave like a dark boiling sea.

Collins blinked. Surely, it was not possible.

Then he heard a tiny cry; it was not inside his head as he first thought. It was near by, and it came from the floor.

"Help me," it whispered. "Please help me."

He allowed his eyes to focus, then cried out as he saw a sticky arm attempt to pull itself out of the seamless, coagulated mass of human life that spread before him like an awful patchwork quilt.

He turned to run, and almost stepped on a pile of rags. A second glance and he thought he saw several pairs of eyes, and a mouth yawning down to become part of a leg.

Later that day, they had to interview the kid again. But by this time he had been joined by another. A face with dark eyes and a nose ring had appeared at his neck, moving as if it was another creature waiting to be born from out of his body. The face spoke in a soft, painful voice, but it was eulogizing about the ultimate experience in belonging, the ultimate experience in bonding.

The big banana.

Liquid friendship.

"Can We Play With the Water?"

"Hello, Jeremy. Can we play?" The greeting came suddenly, from out of nowhere, from somewhere in the dense winter whiteness.

An arm in a sleeve of worn, brown tweed reached forward. A blue woollen mitten covered in glistening flecks retrieved the flat, pear-shaped object from the snow, and offered it back to Jeremy Allan.

"It's called a Ouija board. It's old – very old. Now you can talk to the dead," said the stranger, with a matter-of-fact coolness that made Jeremy feel colder than the nip in the air.

His heart skipped a beat. One moment he had been on his own, preoccupied with his find, the next he had company. He wondered where the stranger had come from.

"People call me Boy," continued the new arrival.

He smiled. His peaked cloth cap was pulled firmly forward; it was difficult to see his face properly. Jeremy guessed that he was probably the same age as himself – about eleven – but it was impossible to tell. He had a "local", country look about him and yet he seemed oddly out of place here.

Boy's clothes hung on a thin frame. They were old

and well worn: an open, brown sports coat with scattered thread-bare areas and a mixture of brightly coloured patches, green flannel trousers which tucked into long thick brown socks. A red woollen scarf puffed out from under his chin, secured within a tatty bottle-green waistcoat. The scarf and mittens seemed to be the only concessions to the bitter cold. He was a strange sight; a dark scarecrow etched from a bleached field of blue-tinged brightness.

Jeremy shivered, his teeth chattered: a combination of nervousness and freezing temperature. The cold did not seem to bother Boy at all.

It was beginning to get dark; there would be more bad weather on the way. The wind gently blew the top surface of snow; delicate ripples of fairy mist scuttled across the garden, anxious to find a new resting place. Jeremy narrowed his eyes and looked long and hard at his mysterious companion. He had been outside long enough, his toes were numb and the wind was beginning to bite. Now was not the time to make new friends.

Boy stood perfectly still. A moon grin grew from ear to ear, presenting a crescent beneath the shadow of the chequered peak. His skin seemed pale, gaunt, with grey-shadowed jowls. His eyes remained hidden. For some reason that he could not explain, Jeremy was very glad of this.

"You scared me," said Jeremy, as he glanced round the garden. "I didn't hear you come over."

Why were there no footprints? He could only have entered through the main driveway gate, but that was some distance from where they stood. The snow seemed unspoiled.

"You live here, don't you?" asked Boy. His head nodded in the direction of the cottage.

"We've not been here long. The house isn't ours, it comes with my father's job."

"I know." The crescent grin returned with the rising sigh of the wind. Jeremy wasn't sure that he had heard the last comment correctly.

"A lot of people have lived here," continued Boy quietly, as though to himself.

Jeremy felt uncomfortable and, strangely, a little afraid. His new companion was as cold as the snow: distant and severe. He seemed to be as much a part of the surroundings as the stark skeletal trees and the hard winter landscape. Motionless, he spoke in clear, bare sentences.

Jeremy had not taken the board back. Boy's mittened hand swept the snowflakes from its surface. It was a light brown colour; the wood grain showing clearly through several coats of old chipped varnish. Slightly larger than a hand, it had a small hole at one end. Boy turned the object over and shook snow off the underside. There were three small wheels, just like tiny castors. He spun one of them round with a single finger; it didn't make a sound.

"Still in working order. After all this time."

"I found it in that old shed. In a box beneath the bench seat." Jeremy pointed towards the top of the garden.

A small timbered building stood behind the thin drooping fingers of a weeping willow. Broken panes of glass, misted by cobwebs, looked out from either side of a porchway. The central door swung from only one hinge and already the recent snowfall was blowing in.

"Ah, the summerhouse," said Boy.

He bent down and cupped some snow on to the board. Lifting it to his face he breathed steamy breath on to the crystals. It was almost dragon's breath.

"See, you can melt it, make water, drink it even. Water!" He began to laugh.

Jeremy wasn't sure what he should say.

Just at that moment the sound of a car horn interrupted the exchange. A pair of headlights flashed from the direction of the driveway gate as a big, black estate car pulled on to the gritted drive and stopped in front of the cottage. Boy pushed the board towards Jeremy.

"Here, take it. It will make us friends."

Jeremy took the object but was far more interested in the new arrival. A smile spread over his face as he waved at the car, holding the board in the air to attract attention.

"It's my dad. He's home early!" he shouted excitedly, as he ran like a leaping hare on a giddy route towards the house.

The snowfall had crept up on them. It was now becoming heavy, the wind frequently whipping the snowflakes into ever-increasing whorls which danced up into the darkening sky. A large, bearded figure in a green hunting cap emerged from the driver's side of the car, a black case in one hand and a cardboard box under his arm. Dr Allan shut the car door with a swift, carefully judged back-kick. He bent his head so that Jeremy could plant a kiss on his hairy-cheeked face.

"Damn this weather," he growled. "Come on, let's get in. What the heck are you doing out in this, any-way?"

"Exploring. Forgot the time. I've been talking to someone." Jeremy turned round to call to Boy. Veils of shimmering whiteness weaved in and out of the space between where they stood and the willow tree.

"Boy!"

The name echoed back across the quiet of the garden, to be caught and carried away by the low moan of the wind.

"There's no one there," said Jeremy's father. "Are you crazy or something? Get in, I tell you, before we both freeze!"

Jeremy stopped in his tracks for a moment. He wondered how Boy had known his name.

Mrs Allan stumbled through the living-room door, her arms embracing several snow-covered logs. She fell towards the large, open fireplace and allowed the load to tumble on to the hearth.

"That ought to do it. Can you shut the door for me? It's awful out there."

No reply came from the corner of the room. Only the familiar rattling sounds, clicks, and then the gentle hum of the current. Jeremy's father sat hunched in front of a computer keyboard. The table lamp cast his huge shadow on the wall behind. Fingers raced over the keys and then momentarily hung in the air, like two large, fat spiders poised and ready to drop. He was sitting at his desk, facing out into the room. The computer screen in front of him faced the corner.

Mrs Allan sighed and looked over in his direction. Behind the screen she saw an intense, dark, unsmiling face. The glare highlighted the silver patches in his beard. The complex information that was being tapped out reflected back on to the glass of his dark, horn-rimmed spectacles: masses of formulae shining out from where his eyes should have been. He looked a fearsome figure, dwarfing the keyboard. A shaggy brown pullover and an occasional growl when he missed a key confirmed his nickname: Papa Bear. His computers were his "little bears". His Disney names made it all the more fun. Less formal. Perhaps less frightening for the job they had to do.

"Speak to yourself, Angela," said Mrs Allan.

She returned to the kitchen and slammed the back door.

"Careful! You'll wake Jeremy," came the call from within the living-room.

"You have got a voice, then. Ears as well," she said, under her breath.

Mrs Allan picked up her cup of almost-cold tea and went back into the living-room, shutting the kitchen door behind her. Adjusting a log on the fire, she sank

into an old red armchair which had been pulled especially close to the hearth. A final resounding tap came
from the desk area, followed by a noisy yawn. Dr Allan
took off his glasses and threw them on to the desk top.
Bright mathematical formulae were replaced by warm
smiling eyes, glowing with satisfaction. He looked
drained, his arms stretched out above his head.

"I'm sorry, honey," he said. "That really needed
revising. I was having trouble. The usual problem with
the new stacks at the plant. The cooling system. I've
developed a new way of checking consistent water
levels – it's revolutionary."

"Oh, good," she said, sarcastically.

He frowned.

"Hey – this is serious. Water's still the best thing
we've got to keep a nuclear power plant cool. No
water and the whole place would go up like fireworks
on the fourth of July! My job's damn important."

She nodded, not completely understanding. Her
husband's frown deepened as he peered at the keys.

"Jeremy hasn't been playing with this, has he? He
should stick to his own computer and all those crazy
games."

"He's a bright kid. He says his own is just a toy."

Dr Allan pushed back his chair and laughed quietly.
"No harm in him playing, I suppose. Good thing we're
not patched into Momma, otherwise Lord knows what
he could do."

He poured himself a drink from a bottle hidden
amongst a pile of textbooks.

His wife looked over at him. Her eyes were restless, moving nervously to a new, red box that sat beside the screen.

"Is . . . is it safe to have that thing here with a child in the house? I mean, what it can do is. . ."

"We've talked this over before," he sighed. "It's special. You need to know the password to gain access. Jeremy can take it apart if he wants to. He won't get in to the main computer at the plant, we're not stupid."

Dr Allan sat down opposite his wife. "Real English, eh? Log fire, country cottage, snowfall. Great." He stretched out his legs. "Shall I fix you a drink, too?"

Mrs Allan shook her head and raised her cup from its saucer in acknowledgment.

"Jim, this will be the last, won't it? It's not me. It's Jeremy. He's lonely, doesn't have time to make friends."

He smiled. Tiredness showed around his eyes. Heavy lids and dark shadows.

"This is the last one. These power plants are virtually running themselves already. We're making history, you know." Dr Allan sat back in the chair and sipped his drink.

There was an awkward silence, then he continued, "I'm also making big bucks, remember. We're getting rid of so-called 'human error'." He paused. "Anyhow, nuclear energy's future isn't that secure; the world may turn on solar energy and wind power yet. We were lucky to get the contract; the whole thing may get dumped next year. Jeremy has just made a friend, anyway."

Mrs Allan looked up, surprised.

"When I got in earlier," her husband continued, "he'd been talking to someone out in the garden. Kid ran off, though. Shy local, I expect."

His wife lifted her finger to her lips. "He hasn't said anything; you know how secretive he can be."

Dr Allan placed his glass down by the chair. "You do like it here, don't you? I told the company we wanted an English cottage for my English wife."

He waved his arm around the room. She didn't answer immediately.

"I think so ... but it seems that we live in a house with one of those *histories*. I meant to tell you, I've had trouble finding a cleaner; local tales, you know."

Dr Allan raised an eyebrow. Local tales – *weird* tales. This was a bonus.

"We've got a spook? That's great! Do we get rattling chains?" He grinned.

She laughed. "Afraid not. The pub landlord's lending us one of his staff, a woman called Dorothy Gibson. Apparently she'll talk our heads off; she collects local stories and knows all about this place. She starts tomorrow."

Dr Allan finished his drink. He thought of washing up and decided it could be left for the "new lady".

"I've had it," he said. "I'm about ready for bed. I just need five minutes to feed Momma."

"Not now, Jim, it's gone eleven," she moaned. "Can't it wait till tomorrow? You live on that thing."

"It's important. If I don't relay it they'll insist I make the trip in, and even though the reactor is only down the road, on a night like this I'm damn glad we've got that special box of tricks. Hell, I can work from home more!" He pulled a face.

"OK, OK." She rarely won arguments. "While you feed *Mother*, I'll check on Jeremy."

"Mother" was Momma Bear, Dr Allan's very special computer at the heart of the power station, caring and protective. Designed to prevent, for ever, the possibility of a nuclear accident.

Mrs Allan wearily pulled herself on to her feet. She wondered whether hot-water bottles might be a good idea and then remembered that they probably hadn't been unpacked yet. Perhaps another blanket on Jeremy's bed would be as good. Suppressing a yawn, she lifted the latch on the stairway door.

"Angela?" he asked, suddenly. She paused. "You didn't say what the problem was with the locals, about the house."

She started to smile.

"I daren't tell you. We have fairies or goblins at the bottom of the garden."

She disappeared up the stairs to the bedrooms.

Lifting the receiver on the bright red phone beside the keyboard, her husband shook his head. He pulled himself from the comfortable clutch of sleep. Installing a terminal link at home had been a stroke of genius – putting to an end the midnight journeys to the plant when anything went wrong.

"Hi. How yer doing? I've gotta feed Momma Bear."

Exchanges were always brief and to the point; they knew it was Dr Allan.

"We never sleep. OK, I know, here goes. This is a quick one. Water pressure: the problem we've had on stabilizing? Net 3790, thirty per cent diversion factor theta. It's a brilliant amendment. I'm running it to check on the earlier program, OK? You know me, persistent. Yeah, I'll be in early a.m. anyhow, snow permitting."

He followed this with a further two minutes of jargon and tapped in a code into the computer. The machine gently purred. A green LED light winked in sympathy. Jeremy had been warned by his mother to keep away from this box. Something from the forest lived inside. It should be left undisturbed.

"That's it. Goodnight."

The arrangement continued to amuse Dr Allan. They wouldn't believe him back home in the USA: a little sixteenth-century cottage in an old Suffolk village could be linked for a few minutes with the heart of the most powerful nuclear power plant in England.

Papa Bear was feeding Momma Bear.

Jeremy was sitting bolt upright in bed. As soon as his mother had left the room, he switched his bedside lamp back on and stared blankly at the pages of his dictionary. The arch of his legs supported the heavy volume. To his left lay a light-coloured pear shape, which had now been lovingly cleaned and polished. A crazy paving of thin cracks glistened beneath the chipped varnish.

He had been right through the book but could find nothing which seemed like the word Boy had used. Wee-jar? Surely not. He had stared at the object for some time. *"Talk to the dead ... make us friends..."* Jeremy remembered the words and could not make sense of them. With a frustrated sigh he heaved the book off the bed and turned round to fluff up his pillows.

Suddenly, the bedroom door whined open and his mother's head peered round.

"Caught you, mister. Bed. Sleep."

"Was Dad feeding the bear?" His mother nodded. Here was his excuse. "He woke me up and I couldn't get back to sleep."

She looked at him disbelievingly and grinned. Jeremy had forgotten about his discovery; his mother frowned as her eye caught the shiny surface.

"Where did you get this?" She gently took it from him, turning it over to take a closer look.

"In a box in that old shed. Can I keep it?"

She didn't answer immediately. Instead she placed it on his bedside table, wheels down, and slowly moved it with the palm of her hand. The castors creaked. Jeremy looked expectantly at his mother.

"I haven't seen one of these for ... well, years. Your great aunt had one, I seem to remember."

"It's a wee-jar," Jeremy announced proudly.

His mother suppressed a laugh. "An Ouija board. O-U-I-J-A."

"You can talk to the dead with it," he said.

She looked up, unsmilingly. "Who told you that?" She didn't wait for the answer. "That's nonsense. It's a game, darling. Just a silly game."

She reached for one of the pencils which lay in a pile by the bed. A piece of paper already lay on the table, filled with circles of coloured scribble. She turned it over and placed it beneath the lamp. Next she put the board on the paper and inserted the pencil in a small hole situated at one end. (Jeremy had wondered about that hole.) Finally, she laid her hand on the surface of the board. The pencil stood upright, seemingly pinning her hand to the table top. Jeremy watched this elaborate procedure with fascination.

There was a moment of silence.

"Go on," he said. "What happens now?"

His mother's voice dropped to a deeper, slower and more solemn tone. It was very dramatic. "Is there anybody there? Whoooo!"

A minute passed by. His heart pounded.

The question was repeated. Outside, the branches of the trees shifted as if in response.

"There you go," she said. "Nothing. That's exactly what happens. Nothing at all. Spirits are supposed to write messages. Call up the departed. But, as you can see..."

She picked up the sheet of paper and held it in front of Jeremy's face. There was nothing there except for the opaque shapes of the coloured scribble which showed through from the other side.

"OK. Now off to sleep, young man, don't go bothering your head with all this nonsense. Your Great Aunt May played with these for hours; used to have dozens of her friends round for tea. She was crazy. Don't mess about with the Great Unknown or you'll go the same way."

Her eyes firmly fixed his for a few seconds and then melted into their usual warmth.

"Computers are much more fun." She cocked her head towards the door. "Ask your dad. Safer, too."

Jeremy smiled. His mother leant over and kissed him on the forehead. The eiderdown snuggled up to his chin. Sleep would be easy. Curiosity was satisfied; he now knew how it worked.

A wave of tiredness swept over him. Final thoughts before sleep reached back to the afternoon. He remembered Boy.

She switched off the light and pulled the door shut. Outside the snow continued to fall.

Momma and Papa Bear slept soundly.

As the rhythm of the wind lulled him into dream, the castors gently creaked.

In the darkness someone called his name.

The door to the stairs swung open. A short, craggy-faced woman in a flowery pinafore stepped into the living-room, a pile of magazines and papers under one arm and an old cylindrical vacuum cleaner trailing behind her. The hose of the cleaner clumsily arched itself into a loop. It had become an uncontrollable snake.

She muttered something under her breath and allowed the combination to fall into a heap beside the door.

Jeremy looked up from the fireside rug where he had been reading. Mrs Gibson let the pile of papers drop on to the cane coffee-table. She coughed and wheezed.

"There you are, love. That's all your papers and things. Sort out what you want and I'll throw the rest out. You kids, like little magpies, hoarders!" She coughed again as she eased herself into the armchair by the fire.

The new cleaning lady was exhausted.

Jeremy had observed that most of her time had been spent in examining the contents of the cottage rather than cleaning them. She had seemed friendly, if a touch starchy at first. The morning had been filled with non-stop stories about the village and its characters. He had also learned about Tom-Tit-Tot and other folk tales: "Most of 'em true," she had told him. Mrs Gibson had known the cottage all her life. It had been years since anybody local had lived there permanently. She called it a "Holiday Let" – always rented. Jeremy had asked why and was answered by the roar of the vacuum cleaner. She wouldn't tell easily.

"The last people here were American," she had shouted above the noise. Then under her breath, "And they didn't last long, either."

Now she was silent, perhaps for the first time since her arrival. Jeremy watched her as she sat in the chair. He thought she had fallen asleep. Her eyelids seemed to twitch as though dreaming.

After ten minutes, her eyes opened wide. For a moment she seemed not to recognize where she was and looked confused. Seeing Jeremy made her relax into a smile of relief.

"I needed that. Only a breather. Tell your mum I'll pop in tomorrow morning to finish, only I've got to get my Bob's dinner and help out in the pub tonight. Tell you another story tomorrow." Mrs Gibson pushed herself out of the chair, picked up the vacuum cleaner and disappeared into the kitchen.

Jeremy collected together the papers from the coffee-table: a mixture of old computer magazines, comics and drawings. He started to devise a sorting system, making sure that everything would be carefully examined. He hated throwing things out. The loose sheets of paper were mainly geometrical designs – computer created. Occasionally a program had been sketched out in rough. Each of these was carefully scrutinized; very few went on to the discard pile.

His hand froze in mid-air above the growing collection of white sheets. It held a piece of paper he did not recognize. With a frown he rose from his knees and walked over to the front window. Holding the paper to the light he stared in puzzlement at the scrawl. His own handwriting was bad but not this bad. It was certainly not his father's.

Jeremy bit his bottom lip and peered out into the snow.

"Bye bye, Jeremy, love. See you tomorrow. I've got a key." The kitchen door rattled open, a bent head peered round the corner and then quickly vanished. The slam of the back door startled him. Mrs Gibson had left.

He turned to his father's desk and flattened out the mysterious sheet of paper. This was a program instruction, but completely unfamiliar. The words WATERDEMON/PASSWORD had caught his attention, followed by some special characters. It was computer language. There was something very odd written below: *Ye thirst, daemon from Fevre Fen.*

At the back of his thoughts somewhere he heard a voice: *"Hello, Jeremy. Can we play with the water?"*

Jeremy glanced over his shoulder. There was nobody there. He sat quite still, considering whether to switch on or not. His father had said that he should really keep off the machine. But it wouldn't hurt, would it? He knew what he was doing after all. He peered across the room, nobody was due back yet.

A few expert manoeuvres booted the terminal into life. Jeremy's usual curiosity and an overpowering love of computer adventure had to be satisfied. This was like a game.

Wasn't there something else feeding his impulse? He had practically run to the desk.

Jeremy suddenly felt restless. He glanced behind him and out into the garden. The blur of whiteness made it difficult to see shapes properly. He searched in his pocket for a handkerchief; he was beginning to feel warm and his hands felt clammy. Again he looked out. He was sure there was nothing there, so why was he looking? What was he looking for? He wiped his hands with the handkerchief and turned to the keyboard. He was filled with a sense of urgency. Carefully, he copied the instruction from the paper, nervous, yet strangely determined. WATERDEMON PASSWORD ACCESS ACCEPTED ran across the screen.

Jeremy typed the message as it was written on the sheet: YE THIRST, DAEMON FROM FEVRE FEN.

The screen went blank.

At first Jeremy thought that there had been a malfunction, but, deep down, he knew otherwise. Gradually a bright orange glow, like an emerging sunrise, crept from the bottom of the screen. It seeped upwards, drawn into the VDU like ink on to blotting paper.

A shiver ran down his back. His eyes stared in astonishment at what he now saw.

The glow began to darken in colour. A soft whisper escaped from deep inside the monitor. It was unthinkable, but it seemed to be alive.

Someone whispered, softly, in time with the hum of the current.

Did it call his name?

It did.

"*I'm thirsty, Jeremy. Melt the snow – make water.*"

He backed away from the screen, knocking the

desk chair sideways. He was afraid the VDU would crack open and burst. The orange had darkened considerably and now filled the screen.

The walls of the room expanded and contracted with the throbbing pulse of the light.

The command had called up something.

Called up.

He remembered his mother talking about the Ouija board. She had said "called up". He grabbed the sheet of paper and turned it over.

Coloured balls of scribble leapt from the page. He suddenly realized this was the sheet that had been upstairs in the bedroom. A small cry caught in the back of his throat as the sheet slipped from his fingers.

The throb of the VDU became faster and brighter, now deepening to a thick red colour. His heart pounded.

The last thing he remembered was the sound of the living-room door opening and the redness on the screen dissolving into a greeting he had heard before:

HELLO, JEREMY. CAN WE PLAY WITH THE WATER? BOY SAID WE COULD.

The room spun round in a kaleidoscope of colour. His tongue felt fat in his mouth as he suddenly felt very, very dry.

Mrs Gibson let out a scream as she opened the door and saw him fall.

Mrs Allan brought a cup of tea from the kitchen and crouched down beside Mrs Gibson. She mumbled a word of thanks and sipped slowly, resting the cup on the edge of the saucer.

"Don't worry, Jeremy will be OK," said Dr Allan. "I've just been up. He's had a shot of something that'll make him sleep. It's excitement, exhaustion and simply playing on computers for too long. He's a computer freak, you see; all those Nintendo things and what-have-you. It's quite common to get a reaction; the flicker on the screen gets to you. Causes dizziness, migraine – the works sometimes. I saw pink crocodiles once. Still do after a couple of drinks."

He laughed, but Mrs Gibson remained quiet and solemn, her nose buried in the cup.

"I'd forgotten my dusters," was all she said.

Dr Allan tried to continue with the explanation. "That's why we usually only work for a few hours at a stretch. But Jeremy. Well, that boy —"

Mrs Gibson was visibly startled.

"Boy?" She had misunderstood him.

"Yeah, Jeremy." His voice softened. "You know..."

"You said Boy?"

"Yeah! What's the problem, Mrs Gibson? Boy!"

The small craggy-faced woman shakily lowered her cup to the floor and pushed herself out of the armchair. Something had upset her. She lifted her coat from the chair and stood quite still for a moment, staring at Dr Allan with a confused expression on her face. At first she hesitated, then it all came out:

"So, you know about Boy, then? He got his hooks

into your lad pretty quick. Jeremy was in a right state. When I found him he just kept right on mentioning the name. Muttered a damn lot of things he couldn't have known."

The Allans looked at one another. They did not understand what she meant.

"He lived here, of course," she continued. "Suppose you know that. Old folk say he was a 'stranger', a bogle. Like the Tiddy Mun, which guards the Fen waters. Only this one was somehow different. There's bin a lot of mischief here, bad pranks up till now. Times were he'd never let any water in the house, swallow it all in a flash. They do that, love the water, these goblins."

Dr Allan stared blankly. "Tiddy Mun? Stranger?" he repeated, confused.

"You know, a bogle – demon from the waters. He got inside a farm lad that lived here. What's the word . . . you know, got *into* him. The lad's dead now, but the bogle ain't. Oh, no. My gran remembers all the things they did to get rid of him. Boy or beast, don't make no difference, he was bad. Get your son out, Dr Allan. He only comes when there's a chance to do harm. It's always bin that way."

She picked up her carrier bag of dusters and looked directly at Dr Allan. "He's after somethin'." Her eyes glazed as her face filled with fear. "What is it, what have you brought? The bogle is back for a reason. There's somethin' here for mischief, got to be a reason, what you got here he's so interested in?"

For a moment Dr Allan didn't know what to do. He hadn't understood a word she had said.

"Look, I know nothing of boys, bogles, beasties, goblins or anything else from your wonderful fairy tales."

"Fairy tales?"

She laughed, then her eyes welled up with tears.

"Should never have come." Mrs Gibson turned and quietly left the room.

Mrs Allan stared at her husband. The back door slammed shut as he shook his head.

"Let her go," he said. It had been an unnerving speech. "What was all that about?"

"I told you we had fairies. I was warned of this at the pub. The landlord thinks they're all crazy. I think I might know what she's talking about. It's some sort of mischievous water guardian, supposed to live in the Fens, but a rogue one took a fancy to the village and pestered some young farmhand that lived round here."

"Pestered?"

She suddenly felt very stupid.

"Possessed him," she mumbled.

"You English sure are weird," was all he said.

At first Jeremy wasn't certain where he was. For what had seemed like a very long time a persistent droning had skipped in and out of his head. His body felt numb; it no longer seemed to belong to him somehow. Although he knew that he was lying flat on his back, the view of the bedroom was from a point slightly above his head.

Memories of the VDU soaking up a dark, red colour flooded back. He started to shake. Everything seemed alive, the air was filled with familiar low whispers as shadows strayed towards the bed.

Slowly he managed to lift his right arm as he struggled to pull himself out of the feathery softness of his dream. A dream which kept dissolving, without warning, into nightmare. Boy's face floated forwards from the shadows, but this time the peak of his cap was lifted.

Jeremy could see the eyes now. Something else was looking out of Boy's eye sockets. The pupils shone bright, glowing with mischief, possessing a sense of purest evil.

Looking away, he again became vaguely aware of the drum of commotion, urgent activity, somewhere in the distance. Something was going on.

The read-out from his digital clock told him that it was gone midnight – he must have slept for hours. He remembered where he was. The muddled noise came from downstairs, the droning gradually focused: the alarm on the modem terminal was urgently crying for attention.

Jeremy dragged himself from the bed. He had to explain. There was danger.

The wail of the alarm was unnerving.

Dr Allan spoke with short urgent breaths. The handset of the red telephone was tucked awkwardly under his chin while he wrestled with a pencil.

151

"Don't worry. No problem. I'll handle it from here. It's a cooling diversion."

He swore as clumsy fingers tapped on the keyboard. The alarm stopped. He caught his breath.

"I'm in. No, it's OK. Keep calm."

The receiver nestled closer into his beard while both hands swiftly moved across the keys, rapping in the password. He paused after access was granted, while a column of figures dropped down on the right-hand side of the screen.

"Come on, come on." He gritted his teeth.

His wife stood anxiously behind him, her thumbnail scraping against the ball of her finger. This had never happened before. She had never seen an emergency.

"I think it's looking good here. Confirm match." He paused expectantly. His jaw dropped. "I don't understand, the core should be cooling. It reads here... It's..."

His blood felt as if it had turned to milk.

"It's become ... it's what!"

He dropped the receiver from his chin and tapped a set of buttons at the opposite end of the modem. The green LED continued to flash. A further panel flipped up to reveal a series of bright green digits which counted away the seconds. His hand, now more positive but still shaky, reached inside and rested there for a moment. A louder, and seemingly more urgent, alarm filled the room. He grabbed the telephone receiver from the side of the desk where it had been helplessly dangling.

"Now, listen carefully. Something's wrong here. I

can't get matching readings. I'm going straight into Momma Bear's belly to cut it off there. . . I know that. Just patch me back. Beta six six, feed four."

Again he tapped a code into the computer, and paused.

The digits stopped counting out.

There was a terrible silence.

At first he thought it was the computer. A purr which slowly changed to a hiss, and then a spit, like a spiteful wild cat.

"What's wrong?' asked his wife.

"Quiet! For heaven's sake, keep quiet! We're right inside the cooling system. I'm controlling the thing from here." His voice trembled.

Mrs Allan's face slowly filled with horror.

"Cooling system? That's water."

"Yeah, lots of it, thank goodness!" he snapped.

For some reason she suddenly remembered Mrs Gibson's words about the bogle. Her flesh crawled.

"The Tiddy Mun!" Panic crept in, her mouth dried. "It wants the water. . ."

He looked at her.

"What do you mean it wants. . ."

He turned back to the screen. Nothing showed. The hissing and spitting grew louder; it was venomous, inhuman almost.

"The creature from the forest," she whispered. "Oh my God, no."

Dr Allan shook his head in disbelief, a desperate groan rising from somewhere inside of him.

Then everything seemed to happen at once. The door to the stairs crashed open, and Jeremy stumbled in, his eyes wide and warning-light red.

At the same time, a long and terrible laugh filled the air. It seemed to burst from the monitor and rush around the room like a huge, hysterical echo. The voice entered the computer screen for a moment, searching for its destination. The screen burned with the sudden brightness of a nova flare for a few seconds. The monitor expanded and contracted like a heart and then, very quickly, the laughter was sucked out into the room and away into the distance. It was like a well-aimed arrow, seeking its target.

"Thirsty!" came a thin, echoing cry.

It shivered on the night air.

"Thirsty! Thirsty! Thirsty!"

The explosion came first. Ripping its way through the tarn blackness of the sky. The house lights flickered. The room was brightly lit from a glow which filled the Suffolk skyline. The perfect snow-white of the garden melted into blood orange as the edge of Suffolk curled its lip like a cornered dog. Along the coastline, klaxon alarms screamed.

The dark red of the computer screen dissolved into a message. The letters shimmered as if they were liquid:

HELLO, JEREMY. CAN WE PLAY WITH THE WATER *AGAIN*?